SCOUNDRELS

A HEIST SOCIETY NOVEL

SCOUNDRELS

A HEIST SOCIETY NOVEL

Ally Carter

DISNEP • HYPERION BOOKS
NEW YORK

First Edition
10 9 8 7 6 5 4 3 2 1
G475-5664-5-12362

Printed in the United States of America

Library of Congress Cataloging-in-Publication Data
Carter, Ally.
Perfect scoundrels: a Heist society novel/Ally Carter.—First edition.
pages cm
Summary: When feisty teenaged thief Kat's on-again off-again
boyfriend, Hale, suddenly inherits his family's billion dollar company,
Kat gets a tip-off that the will is a fake.
ISBN 978-1-4231-6600-9
[1. Inheritance and succession—Fiction. 2. Crime—Fiction. 3. Swindlers and
swindling—Fiction. 4. Wealth—Fiction. 5. Dating (Social customs)—Fiction.]
I. Title.
PZ7.C24263Pe   2013
[Fic]—dc23   2012032405

Reinforced binding

Visit www.un-requiredreading.com

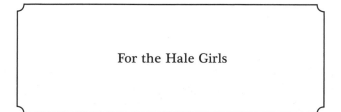

For the Hale Girls

2 YEARS BEFORE
KAT'S CREW ROBBED
THE HENLEY

UPSTATE NEW YORK,
USA

CHAPTER 1

Of all the people who knew about the big house in the middle of Wyndham Woods, very few had ever been inside. For over a century, the owners had been importing their chefs from France, their butlers from England. Occasionally, someone from town would be summoned through the tall gates and down the winding lane to repair a pipe or deliver supplies; but for the most part, the house was like a dragon in the hills, a sleeping legend that barely touched anything beyond its line of trees.

But that never stopped the stories.

The ceilings are forty feet high, some people would say. *The bathroom faucets are made of solid gold.* Every so often, one teenager would dare another to climb the fence and wander through the grounds to get a look at the house, and the trespasser would show up at school the following day with tales of armed guards, Doberman pinschers, and a narrow escape through a tunnel lined with barbed wire.

(The one-way ride in the back of a squad car and the stern call to their parents, however, always went unmentioned.)

But more than anything, people talked about the painting. Sure, most of the town gossips knew only the most basic facts about Claude Monet. For them, it was enough just to imagine what a hundred million dollars might look like, hanging on a wall in the middle of the woods.

And yet no one ever saw it. In truth, no outsider even came close until the night a teenage girl with a long black ponytail and bright blue eyes drove through the town and down the narrow, two-lane blacktop.

No one saw her park the Vespa she had "borrowed" from her uncle Calvin. Not a soul was there to witness how easily she scaled the tall iron fence and landed softly on the damp ground on the other side.

She was not the first teenager to find the narrow path through the woods, but she was the first to stop when she reached the clearing that surrounded the house. She didn't move an inch until the cameras were blind and the guards were distracted, and then all she had to do was stroll to the ivy-covered trellis at the rear of the house. And climb.

At the top of the trellis, the girl wasted no time in pulling a pair of pliers from her belt and clipping the wires that ran, almost undetectable, around the window. A moment later, she was sliding open the glass and crawling inside, as quick and nimble and quiet as a cat.

* * *

The girl dropped lightly onto the hardwood floor, but stayed perfectly still for a long while, waiting for a creak that never came. Even as she crept along the hall and down the stairs, there were no noises of any kind. Not the ticking of a clock. There were no crackling fires or rushing winds. The house was utterly silent, abandoned; and so she dared to walk a little faster, move a little easier, until she reached the big double doors at the back of the house.

There was an ornate desk that had once belonged to a king of England (one of the Georges, rumor said) and a grandfather clock that had been made in Switzerland, a Fabergé egg, and a Hemingway first edition that had been autographed by the author himself. But those things paled in comparison to the painting that hung in the gentle light over the mantel of the fireplace in the back of the room.

For a moment, the girl simply marveled at the painting. She might have been a student in a gallery, a buyer at an auction. It seemed almost enough just to see it—to be so close to something so beautiful. So she stood alone, waiting, until a voice said, "I see you found the Monet."

She startled when the lights flicked on, but she didn't yell or run. She just looked at the boy who stood behind her in a T-shirt with a frayed collar and a bright blue pair of Superman pajama bottoms.

"You're not supposed to be here," the girl said.

"Funny, I was going to say the same thing about you." He smiled like his night had just gotten significantly more interesting.

"You don't seem afraid," the girl said.

"Well, that makes two of us."

Spotlights shone down, and the boy studied her in the manner of someone who is used to looking at rare, beautiful things. Then he jerked his head at the painting and said, "Okay. Go ahead, take it."

He started to leave, but stopped when the girl said, "Yeah, I can have *this* one. It's a fake."

"Oh now, that hurts." He brought a hand to his chest like he'd been stabbed. "Not that it's any of your business, but the Hale family happens to have the largest collection of Monets in the United States."

"Technically, it's the largest *private* collection. And this isn't one of them. This"—she shined a small flashlight onto the delicate brushstrokes—"is a slightly better-than-average forgery."

When the boy eased closer to the painting, it was like he was seeing it for the first time. "No. That can't be right."

"Sorry to break it to you."

He shook his head slowly. "But my grandmother said . . ."

"She lied," the girl told him.

The boy smiled again and whispered something that sounded like *"Hazel is awesome,"* but the girl wasn't quite sure.

"What was that?" she asked, but the boy just laughed.

"Nothing."

"You're a strange kid," she told him.

"Yet another thing we have in common."

This time the girl blushed. It seemed like a compliment, and the way he looked up at the painting told her that the forgery was more precious to him than any old master could possibly be. The girl, however, didn't share that opinion.

Hurriedly, she put her tools away and turned, heading for

her window and the path through the woods. But the boy rushed after her.

"Where are you going?"

"Oh"—the girl laughed—"it's probably best if I don't tell you that."

The boy raced ahead and blocked her way onto the landing. "Tell me anyway."

"Why?"

"So I can go with you."

The girl pushed past and started back the way she'd come. "No thanks."

"I could help."

"I'm sure you'd try." She reached for the window, but his hand landed on top of her own, and right then the glass beneath her palm felt too cold. His skin was too warm. And the girl felt her face flush even against the chill.

He raised an eyebrow. "Of course, I could yell."

She tried to sense whether or not he was bluffing. He had tousled hair and sleepy eyes, and even though he couldn't have been more than fourteen, there was a weariness about him. He seemed thin and pale, and she wondered for a moment if he were seriously ill, like in an old movie where the rich boy is kept locked away from the world at large for his own good.

"No dice." The girl started to open the window. "A Monet I'm willing to steal, sure. But the heir apparent to the Hale empire? No thank you."

"They won't miss me."

"Oh." She laughed again. "I bet they would."

"You don't want to make that bet."

"Why?" the girl asked.

In the moonlight, a shadow seemed to cross his face as he whispered, "You'd lose." Then he moved the hand that had been on top of hers, held it toward her. "I'm W. W. Hale the Fifth, by the way. It's nice to meet you."

He looked serious. He sounded serious. But the girl just eyed the outstretched hand as if it might come with a hidden switch or sensor, and making contact would trigger some silent alarm.

"What do the *W*'s stand for?" she asked.

"Take me with you and maybe you'll find out." He stared down into her eyes and whispered, "I go or I scream. You look like a smart girl. It's your call."

She *was* a smart girl, or so everyone always said. Her whole life she had been taught to be cautious, wise, and most of all, decisive. And yet she stood there in the cold air of the drafty window, completely uncertain what to do. After all, she'd stolen a lot of things in her short life, but she'd never, ever stolen *someone*.

But then again, the girl thought, there is a first time for everything.

So she pushed open the window and climbed out onto the trellis. A moment later, the boy followed; and in the morning, all that the security footage showed was two shadows disappearing into the deep black of the night.

2 YEARS AND 4 MONTHS AFTER KAT TRIED TO STEAL HALE'S (FAKE) MONET

BUENOS AIRES, ARGENTINA

CHAPTER 2

There are few things quite as lovely as autumn in Argentina, Bobby Bishop had often said. And Bobby Bishop was in the business of beautiful things. That was why he had taught his daughter, Kat, how to spot a forgery and scale a fence. It was his voice that was in her ear every time she had to find the blind spots of a surveillance camera or squeeze into a dumbwaiter while reminding herself that claustrophobia is for sissies.

So it was almost impossible for Kat *not* to see the world through her father's eyes. Where would he go? What would he do? And, as the case may be, where would he eat?

"Are you sure your dad's not here?" Hale asked as they stepped into the elevator and he pushed the button for the eighty-seventh floor.

"I'm sure," Kat said.

"Because going to a romantic restaurant with my girlfriend is going to be seriously awkward if her dad is here."

"First, my father isn't here—he's in Bulgaria. I think." Kat furrowed her brow and pondered for a moment before her mind returned to more pressing matters. "Secondly . . ." she started, then seemed to think better of it.

In the past six weeks, she had spent a lot of time editing her thoughts, carefully choosing her words. Laser grids, Kat could handle. But there was a special sort of danger that could lie inside a word like *girlfriend*, so Kat looked at their reflection on the wall of the glossy elevator compartment and tried to steady her voice.

"Secondly, I'm hungry."

Kat hadn't been nervous at all during the planning stages of that particular evening—not when they'd chosen the restaurant or even when her cousin, Gabrielle, had carefully selected Kat's dress and shoes. But as soon as the elevator doors slid open, she heard the music—sultry and low, accordions and violins—and suddenly, Kat was terrified.

In the restaurant, tangoing couples circled past, and the look in Hale's eyes was especially mischievous when he told her, "Oh, I see. You brought me here so you can have your way with me on the dance floor."

"No." Kat pointed past the dancing couples to the solid wall of windows that wrapped around the room. "I brought you here for the view."

Over fifteen million people live in Buenos Aires, and there, on the top floor of the city's tallest building, Kat felt like she could see them all. The restaurant sat on a platform that was built to revolve, slowly moving clockwise past lights and skyscrapers, old historic buildings and illuminated squares. Kat knew it would take exactly one hour for the restaurant to make a full revolution. An hour to talk. An hour to eat. An hour (much to Kat's chagrin) to dance.

"Come on," Hale said, pulling her close. "Humor me."

All around them, couples danced so closely it was as if they were stuck together with Velcro, each absorbed in their own little world, moving like they didn't share the dance floor with a dozen other people.

They were beautiful, and when Kat and Hale joined them, she too forgot that the other dancers existed. Hale was with her. Just the two of them. And Kat actually stopped thinking. She forgot about the jobs they had to do, the things she had to steal. When Hale pulled to a sudden stop, Kat thought he might kiss her. Dip her. Spin her. She was bracing herself, mentally preparing for it all, and she was ready—she really was—for anything but his pulling her close and whispering, "Kat, it's time."

"Right. I . . ." Kat jerked upright and stumbled over the words. "I have to go to the bathroom."

And then she was gone, pushing past waiters carrying trays and women slipping lipsticks into handbags as they returned to their partners. Kat rushed into the ladies' room and stood there gripping the sink and staring into the mirror, trying to catch her breath.

"Kat?" Hale yelled through the door. "Kat! I'm coming in." But he didn't wait for her to answer.

A woman came out of one of the stalls just as Hale burst through the door. She gasped but didn't scream, and Hale gave her a very Hale-ish grin, so the woman hurriedly rinsed her hands and left without a word.

"Are you okay?" he asked as soon as they were alone. Kat

felt her breathing start to rev again. She heard a sound—a *bang, bang, bang*—beating like the telltale heart.

"Kat?" Hale asked.

Slowly, he brought a hand to her face and pushed a stray hair away from her eyes. "Thanks for the dance," he said just as—*bang*—the noise came again.

Kat shuddered and looked out the window. The apartment building she had seen when they'd first arrived was coming into view as the restaurant continued its rotation, so Kat took a deep breath and reached for the glass.

"Are we ready?" Gabrielle asked, sliding into the room, a crossbow, black backpack, and fifty feet of military-grade cable in tow.

Kat nodded. "Let's go."

"You look freaked," Gabrielle whispered while she unpacked their gear and Kat stripped off her dress to reveal the black catsuit she wore beneath it.

Hale was busy at the window, so Kat whispered back, "There was tango," which was answer enough for Gabrielle.

"We're coming into position," Hale said, then handed the crossbow to Gabrielle, who took aim at the building that was slowly moving into direct line with the bathroom window.

"We only have fifteen minutes," he reminded them.

"I know," Kat said.

A knock came on the door just as Gabrielle shot an arrow, sending the cable spiraling across the street to lodge in the mortar above the apartment's window. She clipped a strap from the belt around her waist onto the outstretched line.

"See you on the other side, Kitty Kat," Gabrielle said with a smile, and a moment later she was zooming into the black.

Kat climbed onto the ledge as soon as Gabrielle was clear, but Hale had to help her reach up to grab the cable and attach it to the belt at her waist. She was still dangling there when the knock came again.

"Sir," a familiar voice said from the other side of the door. "Sir, are you in there?"

"Hold on," Hale told Kat, and unlocked the door. "Marcus?"

Hale's valet wore his usual dark gray suit. His posture, as always, was perfect, but there was something decidedly different about the man who stood on the other side of the ladies' room door. He stepped carefully inside and looked at Hale. "Excuse me, sir. If I could have a moment . . ."

"Sure, Marcus," Kat said, still dangling, swaying more than eighty stories in the air. "Take your time."

Hale walked to where Marcus stood, and listened while the butler whispered. Kat couldn't read his lips, but there was no mistaking the look on Hale's face as he turned toward her.

"I gotta go."

"Go?" Kat yelled. She tried to wiggle free of her harness, but the cable was too high and Hale was already reaching for her arms, holding her steady as he kissed her forehead.

"Where are you going?"

"I'll call you in a few days and . . ." He trailed off as if he had no idea what was supposed to come next. "I'll call you."

"You said that already! Hale. Hale!" Kat tried to grab him, but he was out of reach, Marcus at his side, disappearing behind the closing door.

And through it all, Kat's heart kept pounding. The clock kept ticking. So Kat pushed away from the window, zooming into the night.

ONE DAY AFTER
HALE LEFT KAT
HANGING
(LITERALLY)

BROOKLYN, NEW YORK, USA

CHAPTER 3

The old brownstone in Brooklyn was not, technically, Katarina Bishop's home, but Kat was a girl for whom technicalities rarely—if ever—applied. The building itself belonged to a corporation that was a part of a conglomerate that was purchased by a shell company in 1972, and won in a poker game in '73 by Kat's uncle Eddie.

And yet his name did not appear on any titles or tax rolls. Utilities were listed in the names of a half dozen different aliases and paid in full on the fifteenth of every month. As far as the city of New York was concerned, the building was the property of a ghost, a figment, a very prompt and responsible illusion. But Kat knew better. Kat knew the building belonged to a legend.

When she pushed open the back door and stepped into

the kitchen, Kat was certain what she was going to find. The lights were on and the stove was hot. A pair of ancient Dutch ovens sat over low heat, but for the moment, she and Gabrielle were alone as they carried in the small crate that they'd brought from Buenos Aires.

Rich, sweet smells washed over Kat, so she sank onto a chair and put the crate on the table. They'd gone all the way to Argentina for the painting that lay inside, but Kat felt no sense of accomplishment or relief. The couriers would come for it tomorrow, and in the meantime, Kat was tired and drained and happy to be at least temporarily finished.

"Okay, Kitty Kat, spill it." Gabrielle walked to the old refrigerator, threw open the door, and studied the food inside. "I've been beside you for five thousand miles, and, trust me . . . you're in something of a *mood*."

Kat thought about her cousin's words, but she didn't try to deny them. Changing the subject would be futile, and as tired as she was, there was no use in trying to run. So Kat rested her arms on the crate and her chin on her arms, and thought about all the things she didn't like in that moment.

Her head hurt.

Her back hurt.

Her hands hurt (but that was her own fault for doing zip-line work with no gloves).

They were the typical aches and pains of any thief a day off the job, and none of them, Kat realized, could possibly compare to the pain inside her heart, so she took a deep breath and whispered, "Hale left me."

"He didn't *leave you*, leave you," Gabrielle said. "He just made a rapid and ill-timed departure."

"He left," Kat snapped.

"He had a sudden change of plans."

"Do I have to remind you, Gabrielle, that he left me hanging? *Literally.* Are you seriously not furious right now?"

"Oh, I'm mad at him," Gabrielle said. She stirred the contents of the largest pot. "I'm just a little surprised that *you're* mad at him."

"What does that mean?"

"It means, dear cousin, that I wouldn't expect you to be angry. I would expect *you* to wonder *why. . . .*"

Kat had spent twenty-four hours and a very long plane ride across most of two continents fuming at Hale for running off without a moment of thought or a word of explanation. But Gabrielle was right.

Why would he leave so suddenly?

Why would he jeopardize her safety and their job?

Why would Hale, the boy who had been willing to do almost anything to be a part of her world for over two years, suddenly flee without a single clue as to where he might be going?

Somewhere in the house, a door slammed. The floor creaked. On the stove, the contents of the Dutch ovens began to boil. And Kat's cousin raised an eyebrow.

"Are you going to tell him?" Gabrielle asked. "Or should I?"

"Tell me what?" the old man said, but he didn't really stop for an answer. "Do not stir my goulash, Gabrielle."

He moved to the stove slowly, like he'd been dozing in his easy chair and his legs weren't quite working yet. But even with his gray hair and ratty, moth-eaten cardigan, there was something in Kat's great-uncle's eyes—a gravity that could make even a great thief tremble.

"So," he asked again, "tell me what?"

"It's good to see you too, Edward," Gabrielle said in her uncle's native tongue. Then she pulled a noodle out of one of the pots, plopped it into her mouth, and took her seat at the table.

"So, Katarina, what is wrong?" Uncle Eddie sprinkled some oregano into a pot and stirred, but didn't look back. "Was it the access? High-rises can be tricky."

"Access was fine, Uncle Eddie," Kat said.

"The exit, then," he said.

"The exit wasn't a problem." Kat ran her fingers along the rough pine of the crate, and didn't bother asking how her uncle had known the details of the job in Buenos Aires. Uncle Eddie knew everything.

He eyed the crate on the table. Kat could see him calculating the value of the painting that lay inside when he asked, "And so you bring me a box I cannot have, and a problem I cannot solve, is that it?"

"The job was fine, Uncle Eddie," Kat said. "It's just that—"

"Hale ran off in the middle of it."

"Gabrielle," Kat snapped.

"What?" Gabrielle said. "It's the truth. I'm sure Uncle Eddie won't kill him. He'll probably just maim him a little."

"No," Eddie said. "I won't."

"Okay," Gabrielle said. "So he'll maim him *a lot*. But Hale can take it. I'm sure between Eddie and your dad, Hale's just looking at a few broken—"

"No, Gabrielle." Eddie's voice was stern. "I will do nothing of the kind."

"But . . ." Gabrielle gave her uncle a confused glance.

"I value a young man who values family."

"*We* are Hale's family," Gabrielle said.

22

"No." Eddie picked up the newspaper that lay beside the stove and tossed it onto the kitchen table. "We're not."

Kat didn't reach for it. She didn't have to. The headline was big and bold and looming in black and white: WORLD'S SIXTH WEALTHIEST WOMAN COMATOSE IN MANHATTAN HOME.

"Is this . . . ?" Kat couldn't pull her eyes away from the photo that accompanied the words. The woman wore her white hair in an elegant updo, a diamond broach at the base of her neck, as she sat beneath a Monet that, if Kat were to guess, was most definitely the real one.

"That, my dear, is Hazel Hale," Uncle Eddie said. "She is your young man's grandmother."

"She's in a coma?" Gabrielle asked, turning the paper to get a better view.

"She was," Eddie said. "At six o'clock this morning she died."

Kat craned her neck and looked straight up at the building, utterly uncertain what to do. The height would not be a problem, of course, but there was something about the penthouse apartment that loomed over the east side of Central Park that left Kat feeling exposed and fragile. So she shivered, staring up, completely unsure how to find her way inside.

Oh, it would have been easy enough to purchase a bouquet of flowers, throw on an apron, and disappear into the parade of florists and caterers that had been filing in and out of the service elevators all morning. A window washer had left his rig on the third floor, easily within Kat's reach. There were at least a half dozen ways for Kat to access the penthouse, but even Katarina Bishop knew there were some rooms she shouldn't con or break her way into.

Besides, it was the only Hale family residence into which Kat had never been invited. Like a vampire, she felt that it would be almost impossible to enter. So she stayed on the corner, watching, staring at her phone.

"Hey, Hale," she told the recording that answered when she tried his number, "it's me. Again. Like I said in my last message, I'm back in the city and I heard about your grandmother. Hale, I'm so sorry." Kat ended the call without another word.

Maybe he was busy.

Maybe he was sad.

Maybe he was grounded.

Maybe he was still in Argentina, lying in a roadside ditch and calling out her name.

Or maybe he was . . .

"Hale?" Kat said when she saw a pack of men emerge through the building's glistening doors. They all wore dark suits and darker expressions, and they were so uniform in appearance that Kat almost missed the boy among their midst. She stared for a moment, uncertain at first that it was him. She'd seen him in so many situations—playing so many different roles—but Kat couldn't help but realize that the boy who stood before her was someone she had never seen before.

The men were almost at the limo that sat idling at the curb, so she spoke louder. "Hale!"

Every man in the group stopped and stared.

"Sorry," she said. "I meant *that* one." She pointed to the youngest Hale on the sidewalk.

He stepped cautiously away from the others and asked, "Kat?" almost as if he didn't recognize her.

"Hey," she told him.

"Hey," he said back. "How's the Raphael?"

"Fine. Halfway to Mr. Stein and its rightful owner."

"Any trouble?"

"There were dogs," Kat found herself confiding. "We hadn't been expecting dogs, but they took one look at Gabrielle and fell in love, so . . . we made it."

"Dogs and boys, right?" Hale laughed a little.

"Right," Kat said and mimicked his smile. "We missed you."

"Son?" one of the men said. He was tall, like Hale. Flecks of gray mixed among his black hair. He stood at the limo doors, speaking in Hale's direction.

"Just a minute." Hale called over his shoulder and kept his hands deep in his pockets.

"That's your dad?" Kat asked, but Hale acted like he hadn't heard.

"Kat," he said, voice low, "what are you doing here?"

He looked and sounded a world away from the boy who had left her in Argentina.

She swallowed and told him, "I heard about your grandmother. I'm so sorry."

"Thanks."

"I tried calling, but . . . I was worried, Hale. You just disappeared."

"Son?" Hale's father called again.

The first black car pulled away from the curb, and another appeared almost as if by magic.

"Look, I've got to go. The funeral is upstate tomorrow, and we're all going up there today, so . . ."

"Are you okay?"

"It's good seeing you." He headed for the limo, but called back over his shoulder, "Take care of yourself, Kat."

And then he was in the car.

And then the car was melding into traffic and disappearing down the street.

Kat felt Gabrielle come to stand beside her, a cup of coffee in each hand. She gave one to Kat and blew on the contents of the other. "How was he?" Gabrielle asked.

"Different," Kat said, not sipping. Not smiling. "He was different."

CHAPTER 4

Driving toward the big house in Wyndham Woods, Kat couldn't help but think about the first time she'd ever been there. It had been dark, and she had been younger. But the biggest difference, it turned out, was that some places are far more intimidating when you approach them via the front door.

"Name?" the guard asked when Gabrielle pulled up to the gate.

"We're here for the memorial service." Gabrielle gestured at her black dress as if that should be explanation enough. Kat thought that perhaps Gabrielle should have chosen a *longer* dress if she'd truly wanted to send the right message.

"It's a private ceremony." The guard pointed to his clipboard. "Name?"

"We're guests of Hale's," Gabrielle said.

"You're going to have to be a little more specific," the man told them.

"The Fifth," Gabrielle added. "W. W. Hale *the Fifth*."

"You sound very close." The guard put his clipboard away.

"She's his girlfriend." Gabrielle jerked her head in Kat's direction.

The guard leaned down to peer at Kat, then whispered to Gabrielle, "Between you and me, Mr. Hale the Fifth has a lot of girlfriends."

"Well, between you and me—"

Kat leaned across her cousin and spoke through the open window. "Thank you."

"But—"

"It's okay, Gabrielle. We don't need to be *let in*."

It was easy enough to park the car and climb the fence. Even in heels, Gabrielle didn't complain about the long walk through the forest and short stroll across the vacant side of the yard. It was almost like nothing had changed, Kat thought, when she reached the top of the trellis, forced open the window, and slid inside the empty hall. But walking toward the railing at the top of the stairs, Kat immediately knew that she was wrong.

The first time she'd been in that building, it had been dark and quiet. Sleeping. But now the main floor was wide awake. Gabrielle peeked over Kat's shoulder, stared at the crowd that filled the foyer below, and said, "I thought *we* had a big family."

There were men in dark suits, women in black dresses and the occasional veil. And yet it didn't look or feel or sound like a funeral, not with the clinking of glasses and waiters making their way through the crowd with champagne and caviar on silver trays.

It seemed to Kat that it had taken a death to make the big, abandoned house come alive.

"So," Gabrielle said with a deep breath, "this is how the other half lives."

"No, Gabs." Kat shook her head. "This is how the other half dies."

"I guess," Gabrielle said. "I haven't been to a funeral since . . ." She looked away, unable or unwilling to say *your mom*. "Sorry."

"Don't worry about it."

"No, seriously. I'm—"

"Let's just find Hale," Kat said and started down the stairs. Gabrielle fell into step beside her. "We should split up."

"You sure?" Gabrielle asked.

Kat forced a smile. "Absolutely." But as she watched her cousin walk away, she couldn't stop herself from thinking about another day in another crowded room, when she'd sat between her father and her uncle Eddie, receiving guests, hearing condolences. Trying to ignore the fact that her mother was never coming home again.

But Kat didn't want to think about that. She shook the memory from her head and started through the big house, wandering alone, almost invisible, until she found her way back to the painting that had brought her there years before.

"Do you want to know a secret?" someone asked, and Kat jumped, surprised to see a man standing behind her. He had white hair and a trim mustache. The buttons on his silk vest strained against the slight paunch around his middle, but his bow tie was perfectly straight. And behind Coke-bottle glasses, his eyes were bright and clear. Kat suddenly craved fried chicken.

29

"Excuse me?" she said.

The man looked around the crowd of people, who were indifferent to the girl and unimpressed by the painting, utterly unaware that at least one of them wasn't what they seemed.

"It's a fake," the man said, then laughed a laugh that was completely free of pretension, utterly unself-conscious. To Kat, it seemed like the only genuine emotion in that big, cold room.

"Oh, is it?" Kat asked with a smile.

The man nodded. "Hazel had it made after she lost the original in a poker game."

Kat laughed and, like Hale years before, she looked upon the painting—and the woman—with newfound admiration.

"Are you sure?" she said.

"I should be." He leaned a little closer. "I'm the one she lost it to." The man eyed Kat with amused interest. "Forgive me. Silas Foster. Friend of the family."

"Kat Bishop," Kat said, taking his outstretched hand. "Same."

"It's a pleasure to meet you."

"Did you know Mrs. Hale well, Mr. Foster?"

He pondered for a moment before nodding. "You could say that. I met Hazel in . . . what was it? Spring of seventy-two, I guess. Of course, I was just a pup researcher then, and she was the boss's widow." He gave a little laugh. "She got lost her first day on the job and ended up in my lab. Spent the rest of the day hiding in there, plotting her escape. I offered to make her a rappelling harness, but the lab was on the thirty-sixth floor and Hazel was afraid of heights, so . . . she respectfully declined."

"You work at Hale Industries?" Kat asked.

"Director of Research and New Product Development." The man gave a little bow. "I'm the idea guy."

"I like idea guys," Kat said.

The older man cocked his head and gave a laugh. "We get all the ladies. But for some reason I don't think you're here looking for me."

"I don't know," Kat said. "I'm always in the market for a good rappelling harness."

"For you, my dear, nothing but the best."

"But you are right about something. I'm actually trying to find—"

"Young Mr. Hale, I'm assuming."

Kat blushed. "Let me guess—I'm not the only one?"

"Maybe. But you're the one I hope finds him." He gave a wink and walked away, and Kat didn't feel alone anymore in the big room full of people.

"That pervy old dude wasn't hitting on you, was he?"

Kat studied the girl who was coming her way. Her hair was red and her eyes were as black as her dress. She wasn't necessarily pretty, but she was striking just the same, and something about her made Kat stand up taller and blurt, "He wasn't pervy."

She wished she'd created a cover, a purpose. Because the role of uninvited girlfriend absolutely didn't suit her.

"Well, you look . . . nervous."

"No, I'm not nervous. I'm just . . . looking for someone."

If possible, the girl studied her even more closely. She cocked her hip and eyed Kat from head to toe, and in her presence, Kat had never felt more like an outsider, a party crasher, the proverbial thief in the night.

She was just beginning to plan her escape, when the girl said, "You're cute. Who are you?"

"Kat."

"Cool." The girl wrapped her arm through Kat's. "Come on, Cute Kat, we can look together. I'll give you the tour."

Walking arm and arm through the big living room, Kat expected to hear about the history of the house, maybe the story of the Ming vase by the window. She was surprised to see the girl gesture to a woman and three children sitting near the fireplace, then say, "On our left we have the West Coast Hales."

Kat glanced at the foursome. The woman was too thin—her face too tight. Kat was about to ask what was wrong with her when the girl shrugged and said, "Hazel's baby girl thought she'd be a movie star, but instead she married some struggling producer who did nothing but try to get his wife to bankroll movies." She sighed. "She hadn't seen her mother in six years, but she's here now."

They walked through the foyer, and Kat's guide jerked her head in the direction of a short man standing on the bottom step.

"Ezekiel Hale," the girl whispered. "He's part of the European branch; tells everyone he races Formula One cars, but really he's just a gambler. A bad one."

There was a distant cousin who had bought (and lost) a sheep ranch in Australia, a son-in-law who had served time for crimes no one ever mentioned (insider trading), and a son who had shamed everyone by choosing Cambridge over Oxford.

By Kat's count, there were five branches, six divorces, and nine pending lawsuits.

Uncle Joseph didn't speak to Cousin Isabel. Great-great-uncle George's descendants adamantly refused to be in the same room as the children of Aunt Margaret. And everyone thought Alfonzo Hale (a cousin whose mother was an Italian heiress) really needed to get a new toupee.

"And I thought my family was crazy," Kat whispered.

"What?"

"Oh, nothing." Kat squeezed against the wall to let a woman pass (Georgette, granddaughter of George). "How do you know all this?"

"Maybe I'm a spy."

Kat smiled but didn't reply, so the girl shrugged. "Let's just say, if you're young enough and female enough, you wouldn't believe what people will say around you."

"Yeah. I think I would," Kat said just as they returned to the room where the tour had begun.

The people still ate and drank and clamored on about things like dividends and capital reinvestment, and something about the day felt off—almost like Hazel's Monet was not the only forgery in the room.

"Nobody seems . . . sad," Kat finally realized.

"Oh, they aren't sad. They're freaked."

"Why?"

"Hazel was a nice old lady, don't get me wrong, but word at the dessert tray is that the company isn't doing so hot."

"It's not?" Kat asked.

"We'll find Scooter; he'll know all the gossip."

"Who's Scooter?" Kat said just as the girl stopped. And pointed.

"He is."

Kat followed her stare.

And whispered, "Hale."

CHAPTER 5

Hale stood alone in the crowded room, gazing up at the painting that hung above the fireplace. Kat remembered the look in his eyes when she'd told him it was a fake, the way he had come alive. She tried to compare the boy in the Superman pajamas to the young man in the dark suit, but whatever spark had been lit the night they'd met had gone out. She tried not to think that his rightful owners had somehow tracked him down and stolen him back.

"Hey, Scoot."

The redheaded girl stepped toward him.

"Nat!"

Hale smiled and threw his arms around her, and it was like he didn't notice Kat at all. And maybe he didn't, because he just asked the other girl, "What are you doing here?"

"What do you think?" she challenged. "Dad told me about Hazel."

"But . . . I thought you were in Switzerland."

Kat watched the girl tilt her head and choose her words. "Switzerland didn't exactly work out. Neither did France. Or Norway."

"Three schools?" Hale asked.

"Well, technically, five schools—three *countries.*"

"Impressive," Hale said with a nod, and Kat honestly thought he meant it.

The girl reached to straighten Hale's tie. "It's good to see you, Scoot."

"You too," Hale told her, and Kat didn't know what to make of this girl who was calling him *Scoot* and straightening his tie and making him smile.

"Sorry! I'm so rude," the girl said. "I have to introduce you to my new friend, Kat. Kat is—"

"Oh, I know who Kat is," he said.

Kat just whispered, *"Scooter?"*

"So you two do know each other." Natalie crossed her arms and eyed Kat with new interest.

"Natalie's an old friend," Hale explained. "And, Nat, Kat is . . ."

"New," Kat said. "I guess I'm the new friend."

"I didn't know you were coming," he told her.

"Surprise," Kat tried, but Hale didn't look amused. "So, how do you two know each other?" she asked.

"My dad's the family lawyer," Natalie explained. "Before him, my grandfather was the family lawyer. And before him . . . well . . . you get the picture. So I was kind of always around. Scooter here took pity on me, made friends with *the help*. He always was the family rebel." She intertwined her arm into his and pulled him closer.

"You say rebel. They say massive disappointment. . . ."

"You know, I was just thinking about the time with the good china and—"

"Aunt Olivia's Pekingese," Hale said, then broke into laughter. Natalie joined in. And Kat kept on standing there watching, utterly on the outside of the joke.

"So, Natalie," Kat said, "are you back in the States for good?"

"I don't know. Maybe." Natalie shrugged and changed the subject. "What about you two? How'd you meet?"

Kat couldn't help herself. She glanced at the painting above the fireplace, but Hale seemed immune to nostalgia.

"Oh, you know," he said. "Around."

"Cool." Natalie shifted on her heels. Then her eyes locked on a point over Hale's shoulder as a voice rang out. "Scooter!"

"And that's my cue," Natalie said, her eyes wide. "Scoot, I'll see you around. Kat, it's been rad." The girl turned and disappeared into the mourners and out into the garden, before Kat even had a chance to say good-bye.

"Scooter, there you are." A woman was pushing her way through the crowd and toward Hale. She flicked a piece of lint off of his shoulder and told him, "You're as bad as Marianne. Where is she, by the way?"

"I imagine she's taking the afternoon off." Hale's voice was cold. "To mourn."

If the woman had noticed Hale's pointed tone, she didn't show it. Instead, she shifted her attention off of Hale and his nonexistent lint and onto the girl beside him. She looked at Kat's hair, her dress, her shoes, all within a span of a second, deftly taking in everything about her.

"*Scooter* . . ." the woman said, drawing out the word, "aren't you going to introduce me?"

"Hello," Kat said, extending her hand. "I'm Hale's—"

"Friend," Hale said. "A friend of mine. From Knightsbury."

"Oh. How nice." But the woman didn't sound like she thought it was nice. She kept eyeing Kat, looking her up and down. "Where do you call home, dear?"

"Oh." Kat looked nervously at Hale.

"Kat was raised in Europe," he told the woman. "But she lives here now."

"I see," the woman said. "And how do you find Knightsbury?"

"It's better than Colgan," Kat said, knowing that all good lies have their roots in the truth.

"That's what Scooter says." The woman looked at Hale. "Scooter, your father needs us in the study. It's almost time. Say good-bye to your friend."

"Yes, Mother," Hale said, and the woman walked away. He watched her go, and seemed utterly lost in thought until Kat slapped his arm.

"Mother?" Kat gasped. "That was your mother!"

He took her arm and whispered, "You've got to go, Kat."

"I just got here. I thought that I should . . . you know . . . be here for you."

"They're going to read the will."

"They do that at the memorial service?"

"When control of Hale Industries hangs in the balance they do. The business is . . . complicated."

"I see."

"You don't want to be here when all these vultures start

circling." He looked out at the people in the room—at his family. "Go on, Kat. I'll be fine," Hale said, but something in his words rang false to Kat; she wondered exactly who he was trying to con.

"It sounds like your grandmother was an amazing woman, Hale." She thought about Silas Foster and Hazel's fake Monet. "I wish I'd known her. I'm sure everyone just really wants to say good-bye. Hale"—she took his hand—"it's not about the money."

Then for the first time Kat could remember, Hale looked at her like she was a fool.

"It's *always* about the money."

Even before he moved, Kat could feel him slipping away. "Why didn't you tell me she was sick, Hale? I could have—"

"What, Kat?" Hale snapped, then lowered his voice. "What could we have done? Stolen something? Conned someone? Trust me, there was nothing *anyone* could do. She didn't even want to live anymore."

"I'm sure that's not true."

"Of course it's true. The doctors said she could have recovered, but she had a Do Not Resuscitate order. She could have hung on for years, but she wanted to . . . leave."

"Hey, Scooter," Natalie said, reappearing. "Dad told me to find you. They're getting ready to start."

"Okay," Hale said. "Thanks again for coming, Kat," he told her.

"Hale," Kat said, stopping him. "I'm very sorry for your loss."

She meant it. She really did. But watching him walk away, Kat felt like maybe she was the person who had lost something. Hale was always well groomed and well dressed, but that day his hair was parted just so. His cuff links bore the family crest. He didn't look like the Hale who helped himself to heaping bowls of soup in Uncle Eddie's kitchen. He looked like the Hale who belonged to that room, that house.

Natalie draped her arm through his when they walked.

That girl.

For the first time, Kat truly understood why gates and guards had to stand between his world and hers. Never before had she regretted breaking her way into someplace she didn't belong.

"Did he just run off with that redhead?" Gabrielle said, sidling up to Kat and taking a big bite of shrimp. "And answer to the name of *Scooter*?"

"Come on, Gabs. It's time for us to leave."

The woods seemed different on the long walk back to the car, and Kat couldn't shake the feeling that she was forgetting something. Then she stopped and looked at the house.

Someone.

"Hello, miss."

Kat couldn't help but smile when she saw the uniformed man who stood at attention beside a long black limousine.

"Marcus!" Kat cried. "I haven't seen you since—"

"I was very sorry about Buenos Aires. It was most unfortunate timing." He looked at Gabrielle, tipped his hat. "Miss Gabrielle, it's nice to see you. If you don't mind, I have a favor to ask."

"Anything," Gabrielle said.

"Well, I was wondering if I could perhaps drive your cousin back to the city myself."

"You don't have to do that, Marcus," Kat said. "I know it's probably a difficult time for you."

"Please," Marcus said, reaching for the limo's rear door. "It would be a relief to do something."

Kat understood. For a girl who was used to adrenaline and fear, there was no feeling in the world she hated more than being helpless, so she asked her cousin, "Gab, you mind?"

"Oh, please." Gabrielle rolled her eyes, then looked at Marcus. "You can have her."

A second later, her cousin was climbing into her car and driving away without as much as a tire mark to prove she'd been there at all. Uncle Eddie would have been incredibly proud.

"If you will, miss . . ." Kat turned to see Marcus holding open the limo door. For a second, Kat considered sitting in the front, but Marcus was a man for whom tradition and decorum mattered. And so Kat slid into the backseat without another word.

Sitting on the soft leather, Kat couldn't help but wonder how many hours she'd spent staring at the back of the valet's head. He was always there. Never far from Hale's side. And then Kat knew what had been missing from the big house.

"I didn't see you inside, Marcus."

"Yes. I wasn't able to attend, but I was hoping to see you."

"You were?"

"Yes," he said, but didn't offer anything more.

"Did you know Hale's grandmother well?"

"I did. She was a great, great woman."

"Was Hale close to her?"

Marcus nodded. "He was."

"I didn't know." Kat stared out the window. "He never mentioned her to me. Why doesn't he talk about her?"

"The things that are the most precious to us are sometimes the most secret."

Kat nodded and considered the thought. Her family was loud and cranky, a force of nature, moving around the globe like a storm. Hale's family was quiet and fractured, their issues simmering under the surface like a sleeping volcano.

"Marcus," she said, bolting upright when the car steered off the main road and onto a narrow path. "Marcus, I don't think this goes to the highway."

"No, miss. It doesn't."

Marcus wasn't forgetful. He wasn't the sort of man to make mistakes, and so whatever had brought them to that narrow, winding lane, Kat knew it was absolutely not an error.

"We're not going to Brooklyn, are we, Marcus?"

"No, miss." He gripped the wheel and kept on driving. "We aren't."

They didn't go far. By Kat's estimation they weren't more than a half a mile from the main road when the car stopped. She could still see the smoke rising from the chimney of the big house hidden behind the trees, and yet it felt a world away from the tiny cottage with the white picket fence and perfectly pruned roses that stood before her. There were black shutters and flower boxes on every window. An ornate railing ran along a cozy porch, and the whole place looked almost like it had been made from gingerbread.

"Marcus, where are we? Who lives here?"

He turned off the car and reached for the door. "I do."

CHAPTER 6

"I never knew you had a house."

Kat crawled from the backseat of the car and looked up at the man who held her door. Maybe it was her imagination, but she could have sworn he didn't stand quite as straight, there in his own driveway. He looked at her a little more squarely. He wasn't a servant then, she realized. He was a man, welcoming her into his home.

"Oh, it's not entirely mine. I share it with—"

"Marcus? Marcus, is that . . ."

A woman was standing in the doorway, a dish towel in her hands. She had steel gray hair and the same piercing eyes that Kat had seen reflected in the rearview mirror for years.

"Miss Katarina Bishop," Marcus said, "please allow me to introduce my sister, Marianne."

"You're Marianne?" Kat thought about the way Hale's mother had said the name, almost with a snarl. "It's nice to meet you." Kat extended her hand. But Marianne just gaped at Marcus.

"Oh, brother. What have you done?"

Somewhere in the house a kettle screamed. It made a sharp, haunting sound. The woman turned, Marcus at her heels, and Kat followed them into a tiny kitchen with white lace curtains and a tray set out for tea.

"I'm very sorry, Miss Bishop," the woman said, her British accent even stronger than her brother's. "I mean no disrespect. I'm sure you're a very talented young lady. But this is a private family matter."

"You were her family!" It was the first time Kat had ever heard Marcus raise his voice, and she had to do a double-take to make sure it was him and not some well-groomed imposter.

"You forget yourself, brother. And your place. If our father were alive—"

"He isn't."

"Marcus," Marianne said grimly, "this is not our way."

Marcus pointed at Kat. "It's *her* way."

The kettle still screamed, so Marianne pulled it from the flame, but the silence that followed was too loud, and Kat had no choice but to say, "Uh . . . which way is that?"

"I've observed many things in the past few years, miss." Marcus looked her in the eye. "It is not my place to talk, but I do see. I see everything. And after what I've seen, I know that you may be the only person who can help. And so, miss, I would like to hire you. For a job."

Kat could have sworn she'd misunderstood. "A *job* job?"

43

"Yes. There is something that I would like for you to steal."

Marianne brought a handkerchief to her mouth but didn't protest.

"Okay, Marcus." Kat took a seat at the table. "I think you'd probably better start at the beginning."

Never before had Kat thought about whether or not Marcus had a family. She hadn't wondered where he went when he wasn't at Hale's beck and call. But there she was in his kitchen, sitting across from his sister, listening as he said, "Our parents were in service to the late Mr. Hale the Second. Marianne and I were born into this proud tradition, and when our time came, we were honored to follow in our parents' footsteps."

"The family business," Kat added, half under her breath.

Marcus nodded. "Exactly. Our family has worked for the Hales for four generations."

He sat up a little straighter when he said it, and Kat knew that, in his world, that was a thing of great esteem.

"When she was very young, Marianne was asked to care for the new wife of Mr. Hale the Third—a young American woman who had come from . . . shall we say . . . humble beginnings. But who was also very, very kind."

"Hazel," Kat filled in.

Marcus nodded.

"When the new Mrs. Hale came to us . . . well . . . I imagine our world must have seemed incredibly strange to her. The ladies still dressed for dinner in those days. Her new husband played polo with a cousin of the king. And there she was, half a world away from anything she'd ever known, with nothing but a husband who was constantly working."

Marcus took a deep breath. "Well, that's not exactly true.

She had a husband"—he cut his eyes at his sister—"and a maid."

Soon Marianne was reaching for her handkerchief again and dabbing at tears.

"My sister wasn't much younger than Mrs. Hale. There they were, both living apart from their families for the first time. And so Marianne wasn't just a ladies' maid. She was also Mrs. Hale's only friend."

"She was so alone." Marianne's voice cracked. "So, so alone in that big house. She had everything. But she had no one."

"My sister worked for Mrs. Hale for sixty years," Marcus said.

"Sixty-four," Marianne corrected. "I was in service to a fine woman for sixty-four years." She righted herself, standing. "And I know what you think, brother, but I will not sit here and hear her good name slandered."

"So then don't sit. Don't listen," Marcus said. "But that won't change what happened."

"What did happen, Marcus?" Kat asked.

"Mrs. Hale always told my sister that she would provide for her—that she would never have to worry about caring for herself because Marianne would be included in her will."

"Aren't they reading the will right now?" Kat asked.

Marcus gave a solemn nod. "Exactly. Yesterday, we received word that there would be no reason for Marianne to attend the reading—that only those who were *mentioned* in the will were invited."

"Don't be silly, Marcus," Marianne said, summoning her pride. "Who was I to think I'd be included? I'm a ladies' maid. No more. No less."

"Hazel was your best friend, Marianne, and if—"

"It was *Mrs. Hale's* fortune," the maid said, special emphasis on the words as if her brother had grown too comfortable and needed to be reminded of his place. "And Mrs. Hale could do with it what she wanted."

"*This* is what she wanted?" Marcus snapped. "For her oldest friend to be left with nothing? I don't believe it. I do not."

"Marcus," Kat said, her voice low. "Marcus, are you saying . . ."

"These aren't Mrs. Hale's wishes, I'm sure of it. Her family is gathered at the big house today to hear *a* will, miss. But I do not believe that it is *her* will."

"So you think there's . . . what? Another will out there someplace?"

"I do." Marcus nodded. "And I'd like to hire you to find it."

CHAPTER 7

It wasn't like Kat knew what she was doing. She hadn't had time to form a plan, to even know if Marcus was right and Marianne had been wronged. All she knew for certain was that Marcus was still arguing with his sister and, outside, it was a beautiful day. And, besides, her rides—both of them—were either gone or otherwise engaged, so Kat stepped out into the fresh air to collect her thoughts. It wasn't her fault her footsteps kept drawing her through the woods and closer to the big house, one word on her mind.

Hale.

Kat had to talk to Hale. That was the beginning to any possible plan: explain Marcus's theory and find out what—if anything—Hale might know about his grandmother's final wishes and anyone who might want to circumvent them.

For a moment, Kat had to laugh. It all seemed so outlandish, so extreme. But then the big house came into view, and Kat had to remind herself that nothing about Hale's world was ordinary. So she walked across the grounds without another thought. It felt good to have a job. A purpose. And her footsteps felt more certain as she went through the back door and up the stairs.

She threw open one door and moved on to the next. And so on and so on. She kept going until she saw a closed set of double doors, light streaming through the cracks beneath them, and Kat pressed her ear against the wood and listened.

"'To Cousin Isabel,'" a man said, "'I leave the diamond broach that had once belonged to her great-great-grandmother.'"

Kat eased open one door just in time to see a woman throw her hands to her chest. She looked like someone had just named her Miss America.

"So that concludes the issue of the Hale family gems," said the man behind the podium. He had a dark suit and eyes so black there was no doubt in Kat's mind that she was looking at Natalie's father.

He brought his hands together and stood quietly at the front of the room like a preacher at a wedding, waiting for someone to object.

"What about the company?" Hale's father asked.

"Yes, yes." The lawyer shuffled his papers and a few fluttered to the floor. "We are about to that point now, I believe."

"Well, get on with it, Garrett." The Hollywood uncle glanced at his wife. "We have a jet reserved for eight o'clock, and I don't intend to miss it. We've already spent three days on this."

"How rude of Hazel not to die on your schedule," Hale said. His family ignored him.

At the back of the room, Kat dared to open the door a little wider, but no one noticed. The collective gaze of the entire Hale family was locked on Natalie's father. They sat, straight-backed, on folding chairs, waiting. European cousins lined the right wall; distant nieces and nephews gathered on the left. And, at the front of the room, sat two sons, two daughters, and the various offspring and in-laws who had come with them.

It felt like a scene straight out of Agatha Christie, with the country manor's drawing room full of greedy heirs. So Kat peeked inside, staring at the usual suspects.

"Mrs. Hale discussed this moment with me many times, and, before me, she discussed it with my late father. You should rest assured that Mrs. Hale knew the gravity of what she held and the responsibility it was up to her to bestow. She watched her husband accept the mantle of sole control of Hale Industries when his brother passed. She herself took it up after the death of Mr. Hale the Third."

He drew a deep breath. He didn't look like a man accustomed to public speaking as he read, "'Hale Industries is our family's legacy. Our birthright. Our responsibility.'" The attorney adjusted his glasses and spoke directly to the men and women in the front row. "Those were your mother's exact words."

He continued to read. "'My father-in-law gave it to his sons and then my husband gave it to me, and now it is my responsibility to give it to the next generation—to our family's best hope, my greatest faith in the future.'"

Watching, listening, Kat felt a sudden wave of sadness

49

that she had never known the woman who had written those words, and she hated the possibility that there was a traitor in this family's midst, someone who could manipulate the will of the sixth-wealthiest woman in the world to their liking.

"'And thereby,'" the lawyer read on, "'upon my death, sole ownership and control of Hale Industries shall pass to my grandson, W. W. Hale the Fifth.'"

Kat might have thought she'd misunderstood, had it not been for the shocked expressions and stunned silence that filled the room.

"The *Fifth*?" Hale's father asked. "My son? My mother left our company to my son?"

"Actually, Senior," Garrett said, "I think it's *his* company now."

"But he's a child!" Hale's aunt cried.

"And your mother was well aware of that. That is why paragraph eighteen dictates that, should she pass before he is of age, his interest in the company will be held in a trust until he turns twenty-five."

"And who's the trustee?" Hale's mother asked.

"I am," the lawyer said.

Hale's father was up, crossing the room, reaching for the document. "I'd like to see that, if you please."

"Fine," Garrett said. "We have copies for each of you. Hazel's wishes were clear and, make no mistake, her mind was sharp."

"I think company performance of late says otherwise," Hale's uncle muttered, but no one else said anything aloud.

"She knew exactly what she wanted," the lawyer said, and a hush fell over the room as he raised a finger and pointed toward Hale. "And what she wanted was *him*."

CHAPTER 8

When the noise came in the middle of the night, Kat was the only one who heard it. Perhaps it was because her senses were more heightened, her reflexes more sharp. But probably it was just because she was the only person in the brownstone who wasn't already fast asleep.

Gabrielle never even stirred in her twin bed when Kat crept out of the room they shared and down the stairs, inching toward the single light burning in the kitchen.

"Watch the glass," somebody said.

"Hale?" Kat asked. Cold air rushed into the kitchen, and Kat reached for one of Eddie's sweaters that hung on the back of a chair. She pulled it tightly around her small shoulders, shivering in the chilly wind.

"You broke Eddie's window? I hope you can pay for that," she tried to tease, but Hale just ran a hand through his hair.

"I didn't want to wake anyone, so I tried to pick the lock. Have you ever tried to pick Eddie's locks? They're . . . unpickable. So I . . . I'm sorry about the window."

"Hale, what's wrong with you?"

"I haven't been to bed. I mean, I tried to go to bed, but I couldn't sleep. I'm hungry." He opened the refrigerator but barely glanced inside before slamming it quickly shut. "Are you hungry?"

"It's two o'clock in the morning."

Then something seemed to dawn on Hale; a light filled his eyes, and he was moving toward Kat, taking her hands in his and saying, "Not in Rome. You know that little bakery you like so much, I bet it's open. Let's go get some breakfast."

"Hale, I need to talk to you."

"I don't want to talk. Come on, Kat. Let's go get croissants in Paris."

"I thought you wanted to go to Rome."

"We can do both. We can do anything." He pulled her closer. "You know you love me in a beret."

And there he was—Hale. The *real* Hale. Smiling and dipping her low in the middle of Uncle Eddie's kitchen, ready to kiss her like she was the heroine in a black-and-white movie. Gone was the coolly indifferent boy on the street, the vacant shell standing in the corner at the funeral. He was back.

I stole him once, Kat thought. I could do it again. All they had to do was pack a bag and call a cab, jump on a jet and disappear. It could be like it was before Argentina.

"We can leave right now." Hale squeezed her hand. "Marcus will meet us at the airport. Just—"

"Marcus," Kat whispered.

"Yeah," Hale said. "He'll take us anywhere we want to go.

How about Hawaii? We can be on the beach in time to watch the sun come up."

And then Kat pulled away. She forced herself to walk to the other side of the table, needing a barrier—something to keep her from grabbing his hand and running out the door.

"I saw Marcus today, Hale. Did he talk to you?"

"No. He's been staying with his sister. She and my grandmother were very close."

"I know," Kat said. "He told me."

It felt like she hadn't seen Hale in days, and she wanted to fill him in on these strange encounters that she'd had with a boy who looked vaguely like him—to tell him about Marcus and Marianne and the search for a lost will that might or might not even exist. Kat wanted to tell him everything, but try as she might, she couldn't get the words to come, and the longer she stood there, the more Hale's smile faded until, finally, he sat down at the table and ran his hand along the old wood.

"You're not going to run away with me, are you?"

Kat shook her head. "Not tonight."

"That's a shame." He drew a long breath. "This time I think they'd notice."

"They noticed last time."

"You're right." He gave a low, dry laugh. "But this is the first time they'll care."

"Hale—"

"Hazel disinherited my parents, Kat," Hale finally said. "My aunts and uncles, too. Sure, she gave away some jewelry and some paintings—the houses. But she didn't give them a single share of Hale Industries." He huffed. "Ever since Hazel got sick, that's all Dad has been able to think about. His mother was dying, and all the man could talk about was how

53

hard it was going to be to buy his brother and sisters out of the company."

Hale took a deep breath. "She disinherited everyone," he said, as if trying to convince himself that it was true. "And she gave it all to me."

The moonlight sliced through the broken window and across his face. He didn't look like a boy who'd just inherited a billion-dollar corporation. He looked like a boy who wanted his grandmother back.

"Why would she do that? Why would she pick me?"

It was supposed to be rhetorical, but Kat couldn't help herself; she thought about the question—saw it in the light of everything Marcus had said. And in that moment, she knew that Hale being the heir was no mistake, no coincidence. It was an all-important part of the con, Kat was certain, as she whispered, "You're a minor."

So often in life, Katarina Bishop forgot that she and her crew were teenagers, that in the eyes of the law and society itself, even W. W. Hale the Fifth was a lesser citizen. It had often been an asset, but it had never made her a mark before, and right then she hated being fifteen.

"Like I wasn't a black sheep enough before, now I'm the kid who stole their inheritance. They can't even look at me. My aunts and my uncle . . . My own parents hate me."

"I'm sure they don't hate you."

He shook his head as if she were the most naive girl in the world. "Of course they do."

It's not about you, Kat started to say. She wanted to tell him that there might be something wrong—that if she was right, then he was just a small piece in a much, much larger puzzle. She was opening her mouth to speak—the words were almost out—when a broad smile stretched across Hale's face.

"But do you want to know the crazy part, Kat?"

"What?"

"I don't care." He laughed a little. "There was only one person in my family I ever trusted. Turns out, I'm the person she trusted, too."

And then Kat's words disappeared. They evaporated into the cold air that blew through the broken window, and she couldn't bring herself to tell him that Hazel's grand, final gesture might be nothing more than a lie.

"My grandmother loved me, Kat." He smiled wider. "She chose *me*."

There Kat was, in the center of her world, and she tried to imagine what it would be like to never be respected, accepted. Loved. Kat had always belonged in Uncle Eddie's kitchen, and she tried to wrap her mind around what it would be like to be the boy who had never been given a place at his family's table.

"I'm sorry." Hale took her hand. "You wanted to tell me something?"

She did want to tell him something—so many things. But the words didn't come. So she rose and walked around the table, brought her hand to his face, and kissed him.

"Why shouldn't she choose you?" Kat forced a smile. "I did."

After he'd closed the door and disappeared down the dark street, Kat was left alone in the sleeping house, wondering if she'd made the right decision. It wasn't until she turned and started for the stairs that she realized that, no, she wasn't alone after all.

"Tell me everything." Gabrielle crossed her arms and blocked the way. "Tell me everything, now."

CHAPTER 9

"Hello, Marianne," Kat said the following morning. The tiny yard was wet with dew and the sun was still low, the house shrouded in the shadows of the woods. But as soon as the woman opened the door, Kat knew she hadn't been sleeping. Marianne's eyes were bright and clear as she regarded the two girls who stood on her stoop, mulling over the consequences of asking them inside.

"Marcus isn't here," she told them.

"That's fine," Kat said. "This is my cousin Gabrielle. If it's okay, we'd like to talk to you." But the woman didn't speak or move. "Please, Marianne. We think that maybe Marcus is right. And we think maybe you're not the only one who was affected."

Kat watched her weigh the words, consider her options,

then slowly push the door open and gesture for them to follow.

Kat and Gabrielle sat on the floral sofa while Marianne went to the kitchen and made tea. It was a simple house, but lovely. And Kat imagined that within those twelve hundred square feet, the brother and sister could pretend they'd never really left England.

"I'm sorry I'm such a mess," Marianne said when she returned. She placed the tray on a low table in the center of the room. From where Kat sat, she couldn't see a single hair out of place on the woman's head, but Marianne patted at them just the same. "I've worked every day since I was fourteen. I'm not quite myself without a job to do."

Kat nodded. "I know the feeling."

"Yes, miss," Marianne said. "I don't doubt it."

"Where is Marcus?" Gabrielle asked.

"He's back with young Mr. Hale today. Marcus offered to stay with me, but I told him that he should go. That boy will be needing Marcus now more than ever."

"So you know . . ." Kat said.

"That young Mr. Hale inherited the company?" the woman filled in. "Yes. I heard." She smiled. "I was very happy to hear that. His grandmother loved him so."

"Did that surprise you, Marianne?" Kat asked.

"Oh, I suppose I had just assumed it was going to be divided among her children, but . . ." She trailed off and brought a hand to her lips. "I just don't know. He's so young."

Kat nodded. "There will have to be a trustee to oversee things until he turns twenty-five."

The woman furrowed her brow and asked, "Who?"

"Garrett. The lawyer."

Try as she might, Kat couldn't quite decipher the look

that crossed Marianne's face. There was something there, though—a flash so fleeting that a normal person would have never seen it—and Kat thought for a moment that Marianne might have made a most excellent grifter.

"What is it, Marianne?" Kat asked.

"Nothing," she said, pulling her shawl more tightly around her shoulders.

"Oh, I think there's something," Gabrielle said, her voice cold.

"Gab," Kat warned, but Gabrielle had her sights set on the woman.

"Marianne, you worked for Hazel for half a century, and now you know something. Don't try to deny it. You know something, don't you?" Gabrielle asked. But the woman didn't answer.

"Marianne?" Kat asked softly. "What is it?"

Marianne recoiled and shook her head. "It's nothing. A crazy notion. You wouldn't believe me if I told you."

Kat and Gabrielle leaned closer and, in unison, said, "Try us."

"I just can't imagine that Mrs. Hale would name Garrett as the trustee. That's all."

"Didn't she like him?" Gabrielle asked.

"No." Marianne laughed. "Hazel wasn't one to gossip, but I could tell she couldn't stand the man. In fact, I thought she was going to fire him."

"Then why didn't she?" Gabrielle asked.

Marianne's eyes grew moist. When she spoke again, her voice was almost a whisper. *"She died."*

"It's okay," Gabrielle said. "Just tell us what happened."

Marianne drew a deep breath and spoke softly. "A week

or so ago, Mrs. Hale asked me to call the office and schedule a meeting with Mr. Garrett and a few members of the board. I did as she asked, but that night she grew ill, and then . . . well, she never made it."

"Marcus said that he thought there was another will," Kat said. "One that contradicts the one they read yesterday."

"*He* thinks so," Marianne said. "And maybe there is. I don't know anything for certain." For the first time, Marianne smiled. "Mrs. Hale *was* a bit of a pack rat. And a worrier. People who enter this world with nothing always are. If there was another will, she probably would have kept a file for herself."

"Where?" Kat asked. "If it exists, where do you think it would be?"

"Did she have a safety deposit box?" Gabrielle tried. "A safe, somewhere? Maybe a—"

"It's in her desk," Marianne said suddenly, cutting Gabrielle off. "If she has another will, it would be in her desk in London."

"Cheerio, Kitty Kat," Gabrielle said in her best Cockney accent, but her smile faded as soon as she read the expression on her cousin's face. "What's wrong?"

"It's just that . . . if we were running this con"—Kat cut her eyes at Marianne—"which we *aren't*. But if we were, the first thing I'd do is destroy any copies of the old will. I want you to know that, odds are, whoever is behind this has already done just that."

"Oh, I wouldn't be so certain."

"Why?" Kat prompted.

The woman smiled. "Because the desk where Mrs. Hale stored her most important papers was made by Alexander Petrovich."

"It's a Petrovich puzzle desk?" Kat asked.

Marianne gave a wide, knowing grin. "Someone could empty every drawer in it and still miss the hidden compartments. If the will exists, there's a good chance a copy of it is still there."

Neither girl spoke on the long drive back to Brooklyn. It was midday and the sun was bright. Spring flowers dotted green fields beneath a bright blue sky. It was almost like a painting. Kat was half tempted to steal it. But when they reached the brownstone's stoop, their shadows fell across the door, and it was like a spell was broken. They could no longer pretend that nothing was wrong—that they didn't have work to do. And when Kat opened the door, she wasn't surprised to hear her uncle's deep voice echoing through the house.

"Katarina! Gabrielle! Come in here."

For a moment, Kat was certain she was in trouble. She glanced at Gabrielle, and together the two said, "Yes, Uncle Eddie?"

"Sit down," he said, pointing toward the old mismatched chairs. "We need to talk about Katarina's young man."

"I'm sorry about the window, Uncle Eddie. I'll get it—"

"The window can be fixed, Katarina. I'm far more concerned about him."

"I know." Kat nodded solemnly. "Me too."

"So . . ." There was a pile of potatoes on the counter, and Eddie took a knife and began to peel. "It seems there is a great deal of mystery surrounding why the late Mrs. Hale would leave a billion-dollar corporation to a teenager and nothing to her oldest, dearest friend."

"How did you know that?" Kat asked.

"I hear things," Eddie told her.

But Kat knew better. Kat knew Eddie heard everything.

"If the butler is correct, then this is a most impressive con."

"We know," Gabrielle said, and Eddie talked on.

"It would have to be an inside job. Simple, but not easy."

"We know," Gab said again, but Eddie acted like he hadn't even heard her. Kat couldn't tell if he was frightened or impressed, and she felt a little bit of both as she sat silently watching her uncle peel potatoes, stripping away the skins.

"What did the maid say?" Eddie asked.

"There might be another will in London. Maybe." Gabrielle gave a shrug.

"You will try to retrieve it?" Eddie looked directly at Kat, but she felt anything but certain.

A thousand doubts swarmed inside her mind. What if Hale found out? What if Marianne was wrong? And, worse, what if Marianne was right? And what if Hale never forgave her for proving it?

So Kat twisted her hands and told her uncle, "It might be a wild-goose chase."

"I've chased more for less," her uncle said.

"Marcus could be wrong about everything."

"He is not the sort of man who makes mistakes."

"But—"

Her uncle's hand came down, cutting her off, as he asked, "You do a great many things for strangers, Katarina. What are you willing to do for your friends?"

2 DAYS AFTER THE READING OF THE WILL

LONDON, ENGLAND

CHAPTER 10

The best-kept secret in London had to be City Airport, Kat had always thought. Smaller than Heathrow and more central than Gatwick, it was like flying into a small town until you looked out the window and saw Big Ben and the Tower of London below. It was as good a place as any for a teenage thief to go through customs and descend into the very place where she'd pulled off the biggest job of her career only a few months before.

But that didn't mean Kat had to like it.

Stepping through the airport's sliding doors and out into the dreary London day, Kat sensed a nagging doubt in the back of her head, a tiny voice that kept telling her something wasn't quite right. Or maybe it was just Gabrielle.

"Commercial, Kitty?" Gabrielle asked, annoyed. "Really? We just *had* to fly commercial. . . ." Gabrielle shifted on the tall boots that descended from beneath a very short skirt printed with the Union Jack, and moved her head from side to side, popping her neck—the universal gesture for *long flight*. "For the girlfriend of a gazillionaire, you really don't know how to travel."

"We weren't exactly traveling on official gazillionaire business."

"We could have been," Gabrielle said, "if we'd told Hale where we were going. And why."

"Don't start, Gabs," Kat said.

"What?" Her cousin gave an innocent shrug, slid her dark glasses on, and walked toward a waiting cab. "Come on. This is our ride." Gabrielle opened the door and crawled into the black car. Kat followed. She sat her bag at her feet and spoke to the driver.

"Hi, we're going to—"

But before she could finish, the car zoomed off, throwing her against the seat back. Her suitcase toppled over, smashing against her foot.

"Ouch!"

"Sorry about that, Kitty," the driver said.

"Hamish?" Kat cried.

"Should have warned you to . . . Hold on!" said Angus, Hamish's brother, from the passenger seat as Hamish spun the wheel and sent the cab careening into traffic.

Kat sat breathless while the car swerved around big red double-decker buses and in front of men in suits riding bicycles with briefcases tied to handlebars. Outside, it started to rain, and Kat heard the water pelting against the car as Hamish turned down a narrow cobblestone alley—entirely too fast, in Kat's opinion.

"So, guys," she said, leery and glaring at Gabrielle, "I wasn't expecting to see you on this trip."

"What?" Gabrielle asked. "I can't make an executive decision? Besides, everything is better with Bagshaws."

Kat was beginning to seriously question her cousin's definition of "better" when Angus looked over the front seat. "So, between you and me . . ."

"And me," Hamish added.

"How rich is ol' Hale these days?" Angus finished.

"Guys." Kat gave an exasperated sigh. "He's Hale. Hale is just the same as he was before, just—"

"Richer," Gabrielle said. "About a million times richer."

In the front seat, Angus gave a long sigh. "I always did like that boy."

"So true," his brother said. "So, so true."

Then Hamish spun the wheel again. Dark alley gave way to the glow of neon through the foggy windows, and Kat knew immediately where they were. She couldn't help herself: she thought about the last time she'd been in Trafalgar Square— the long ride in the back of a mobster's car. Blackmail photos and death threats. She was beginning to question why she'd thought it was so important to come back to England.

"What's wrong, Kitty?" Angus asked.

Kat reached out to touch the window. "London makes me nervous."

"Don't worry, Kat," Hamish said. "You're about to feel much, much worse."

The skyscraper was new, right next to the Thames. Someone said something about it being the tallest building in Europe, but Kat wasn't really in the mood to care. She just stood quietly in the elevator, and when they finally reached the penthouse apartment, Kat was more than a little relieved to see that Gabrielle had a key.

"Who owns this apartment?" Kat asked.

"Carlos," her cousin said, pushing open the door and stepping inside. A staircase ascended into a second story. A modern kitchen covered the right side of the space. It was all steel and chrome and glass. Even though Kat was back in London, it felt like a different hemisphere—different century—from the country estate where they'd stayed when planning the Henley job.

"And Carlos is . . ."

"About to be step-daddy number five," Gabrielle told her. She cocked a hip. "He's Cuban."

"How nice for him," Kat said, and followed her cousin into the towering, frigid room.

Rain ran down the tall glass windows, and the flames from the long sleek fireplace didn't even begin to fight the chill. Suddenly, Kat craved soup and a warm kitchen. She felt a long, long way from home.

"So tell me." Kat dropped her bags and spun on the Bagshaws. "What exactly is wrong?"

"There's a bathroom down there," Gabrielle said. "If you want to try to do something about . . . this." She gestured to Kat's hair. Kat ignored her.

"Guys, what's going—"

"Oh good, you're here."

"Simon," Kat said, looking up at the boy descending the stairs, a laptop under each arm. As happy as she was to see him, another emotion boiled to the surface. "What are you doing here? What are all of you doing here? Gabrielle—"

"Don't be mad at dear, sweet Gabrielle, Kitty," Angus said, even though Kat was fairly certain that Gabrielle had never been *dear* or *sweet* a day in her life. "It's hard out there for a couple of lads trying to find honest work."

"Honest?" Kat asked.

"Or honestly dishonest, as the case may be," Hamish said.

Kat turned to Simon. "I thought you were doing a PhD program at Cambridge."

"Oxford." Simon blushed. "And I didn't find the academic setting as challenging as I'd hoped."

"University girls don't date teenage geniuses," Hamish translated.

"Okay. Great. So Simon's a dropout and you two are . . . here." She pointed at the Bagshaws. "But guys, it's not a big job. I mean, we just need to get into Hale's grandmother's flat. That's not exactly—"

"Oh, the flat is nothing." Angus pulled an apple from a bowl on the marble counter and took a big bite as he said, "Hale's aunt inherited the place, and she's kind of . . ."

"Unpleasant," Hamish filled in while Angus provided his own (far less flattering) word.

Simon talked on. "So the whole staff is turning over. Getting in and out with all the chaos would be a cakewalk."

Kat studied the solemn faces that were looking back at her. "So that means the problem is . . ."

"The desk is an original Petrovich." When Simon spoke, he began to subtly vibrate in excitement. "I mean, a *real* Petrovich. Did you know that Catherine the Great herself discovered him and—"

"Simon," Gabrielle said. "Focus."

"Sorry." He pulled his thoughts back together. "It's just,

69

I've always wanted a Petrovich," Simon said. "Those desks are like works of art."

"And *that*, dear cousin, is the problem, because there is going to be an exhibition of Petrovich's finest work at . . ." Gabrielle let the words drag out long enough for Kat to guess.

"The Henley."

"Yep," Hamish said. "Welcome to London."

"Can't we get in before the museum takes possession?" Kat asked.

Angus gave an exaggerated sigh. "The Henley picked up the desk three days ago."

Gabrielle nodded, then hopped onto the counter and crossed her long legs. "And so that means . . ."

"We have to rob the Henley," Simon said.

Kat sank onto a truly uncomfortable sofa. "Again."

3 DAYS AFTER THE READING OF THE WILL

LONDON, ENGLAND

CHAPTER 11

Despite the fact that Alexander Petrovich was a member of the court of Catherine the Great, he was not a royal. Even though he apprenticed with Moscow's finest carpenters, he was far more than a mere craftsman. No, what Petrovich really was was an artist. And like most of the great artists in history, his work eventually wound up at the Henley.

Oh, there was no denying that things at the Henley had changed in the past few months. From the moment a small business card bearing the name *Visily Romani* had appeared in a locked (and supposedly secured) wing of the museum, many said that the Henley's luck had shifted.

First there were headlines. Later, there was fire and chaos. And when the smoke finally cleared, a group of frightened schoolchildren was found locked in a gallery, and Leonardo da Vinci's *Angel Returning to Heaven* was gone. And soon the Henley's reputation as the most exclusive (not to mention secure) museum in the world had vanished.

But months passed. The smell of smoke faded. And now the *Angel* and Romani and perhaps even the children themselves were gone for good, and things were finally returning to normal.

Or so the Henley thought.

It was a rare sunny day in London when Kat stood in the courtyard outside the museum's main doors, staring up at the atrium made almost entirely of glass. Kat's life had changed inside those walls. Walking in, she had been Uncle Eddie's great-niece, Bobby Bishop's daughter. But walking out, Kat had had a piece of Holocaust art under her arm and a new purpose to her step, and she never looked back.

So it should have felt nice walking through that massive atrium and back into the sight of her former glory. But it didn't.

For starters, there was the wig that Gabrielle had purchased and Kat had been afraid not to wear. Then there were the heels her cousin had forced her into and the thick glasses that completed her disguise. But more than anything, there was the terrible sense of dread that filled her gut as she walked past the wall where *Angel Returning to Heaven* had once hung.

So, needless to say, Kat was glad for any excuse to walk in the other direction. Glass sculptures dangled from the tall ceilings, floating in a nonexistent breeze. But when Kat turned a corner, she had no choice but to stop dead in her tracks.

"Hey, Kat?" Gabrielle asked through the comms unit in her ear. "Are you at the Petrovich room yet?"

Kat said nothing.

"Kitty . . ." Hamish tried again. "Kitty, are you—"

"Guys, we have a problem," Kat finally managed to mutter.

"What?" Gabrielle said.

"The Petrovich exhibit isn't *in* a room."

Kat looked down the long promenade, at the desks arranged in the center of the massive corridor, each surrounded by velvet ropes. Guards were stationed on either end of the long hall filled with school groups and tourists and art lovers just out for the afternoon. *"It isn't in a room!"* she spat in frustration.

"Okay, Kat. Just calm down," Gabrielle was saying, but Kat couldn't answer—couldn't even pull her eyes and mind away from the desk that was inches away. There was nothing but a soft velvet rope between Kat and the beautiful mahogany piece that bore the label FROM THE ESTATE OF HAZEL HALE.

Part of Kat wanted to jump over the rope, kick and claw at the desk—break it into a million pieces if she had to. Find the will, and be gone. Of course, she knew a basic Smash and Grab would never work at the Henley. Still, a part of her wanted to try.

"Are you ready, Kitty?" Hamish asked. "Kat?"

She took a deep breath. And said, "I've seen enough. Let's go."

CHAPTER 12

If Carlos's apartment had seemed cold to Kat when she first saw it, then the following night the room felt absolutely frigid.

The London skyline was perfectly clear through the tall glass walls, with the London Eye spinning around and Big Ben overlooking the House of Commons. Kat was a hundred stories above it all, hidden in a fortress of steel and glass, and yet she couldn't help feeling entirely too conspicuous, like anyone and everyone could see what they were doing. Even though Hale was on the other side of the Atlantic, Kat still wished she could draw the blinds.

"So what do we know?" Gabrielle asked. In the reflection of the windows, Kat saw her cousin sashay into the room.

"They've changed their guard patterns," Hamish said.

"And most of their guards," Angus added. "Which I don't

mind at all, I can tell you. One of those blokes was bound to remember me, handsome as I am."

"Simon?" Gabrielle asked, but he just kept staring at the computers spread out on the table in front of him. It was like he didn't hear a thing.

"Simon!" Gabrielle shouted.

"Yes." He bolted upright, startled. "Yeah. Okay. Do you want the good news or the bad news?"

"Good," everyone but Kat said in unison.

"Oh." He deflated.

"What?" Kat asked.

"I don't really have good news; I was just hoping to soften the bad," he said.

"Just tell it like it is, Simon," Kat said.

"Well, they've changed their cameras since we hit them last fall," he began.

"That's good news there, isn't it?" Hamish tried.

"These have facial-recognition software," Simon added. "So . . . no. But I don't think they have any records of our faces from last time, so . . . hey . . . that's good news!"

He seemed so happy, so proud of himself. And Kat couldn't be still a moment longer. She started to pace.

"Cat in the Cradle?" Gabrielle said.

"We don't have Hale," Hamish said.

"You could do it," Gabrielle challenged.

"Do I look like a classically trained violinist to you?" he asked, and Gabrielle didn't broach the subject again.

"Then what about an Ace's Wild?" Simon said.

Angus scooted forward. "*With* a little Count of Monte Cristo?"

"Exactly," Simon said, excited.

"Yes." Gabrielle crossed her arms. "That is the perfect way to remind everyone at the Henley that *we* were the kids locked in a supposedly abandoned gallery when the *Angel* was stolen."

"Maybe that back door into their computer system is still there," Simon said, and Kat could practically hear his palms sweating. "If it is, maybe I could—"

"Chill, Simon," Gabrielle said, looping an arm around his shoulders. "Breathe."

"But—" he started, and Kat cut him off.

"They closed that back door before they plastered over the nail the *Angel* hung on. No one is ever going to use that again."

Simon hung his head, mourning the fact that a most excellent security breach had had to die for their last mission to live.

The silence stretched out, wrapping around them like the city skyline on the other side of the glass. It felt for a moment like they were floating, suspended, flying down the Thames. Kat prepared herself to feel the crash.

"'Course, we could do this the easy way." Angus sounded like he'd been waiting hours for someone—anyone—to state the obvious.

"An *easy* way?" Kat said. "To rob the Henley?"

"An easy way to get into the *Hale desk* in the Henley." Hamish was up and walking purposefully across the room. "If only we knew someone. Someone named . . ."

"Hale?" his brother guessed.

"Precisely," Hamish said.

"No," Kat told them with a quick shake of her head.

"I know ol' Hale is busy, Kitty Kat," Angus talked on, "but he'd come if you called him."

"No," Kat said, walking toward the coffeepot in the kitchen. She was tired of being cold. "I won't call him."

"Fine, then," Angus said, following. "I'll call him. I bet even *the* Hale of Hale Industries would be glad to jump on that corporate jet and . . . what's the word?"

"Jet," his brother supplied.

"Yes, jet over to help. He'd be—"

"No!" Kat snapped, then drew a deep breath. Her hands began to shake, so she set the coffeepot down. "Hale can't help, okay? He just can't."

"And why would that be?" Simon asked.

"Because, technically, Hale doesn't know we're here," Gabrielle said.

Kat felt the truth of it wash around the room until, finally, Angus had to ask, "Then who does know?"

"Marcus," Kat said. "And Marcus's sister."

"And Uncle Eddie," Gabrielle added, defiant. "This time, Uncle Eddie totally knows. And approves."

Angus eased forward. "What's going on, Kitty?"

"It's complicated."

"Try us," Hamish said.

Kat couldn't help herself. She risked a glance at Gabrielle, who nodded. "It's just . . ." Kat spoke slowly. She had to build up the courage and momentum to say, "It's just that Hale might not be the real heir. Okay? It might all be a con."

"A con?" Simon asked. "Like a Prodigal Son?"

"No." Kat shook her head. "Well, not exactly. We think there may be a different will. A real will that gives the company to someone else. And it may be in that desk."

The words washed over them all, the truth settling down around them. It seemed to take forever for Angus to say, "Call me heartless, but isn't the current will . . . you know, the one that gives our friend Hale about a billion dollars . . . a *good* will as far as we're concerned?"

It wasn't an easy question, so Kat wasn't in a hurry to answer. She sank onto the sofa and thought about Marcus and Marianne and finally the look in Hale's eyes when he'd told her that the only member of his family he'd truly loved had trusted her most precious possession to him and him alone.

"I don't know, Angus. I really don't. I just know I need to find out the truth."

"Then we find the truth," Simon said. The Bagshaws nodded.

"How much time do you think you'll need with the desk, Kitty?" Hamish asked.

Kat placed her elbows on her knees and thought. "I honestly have no idea."

"The world record for cracking a Petrovich is two minutes fourteen seconds," Simon said. When the others gaped at him, he shrugged and added, "There are tournaments. I'm a fan."

"So the low end is two minutes," Gabrielle said.

"Not counting the exit," Simon filled in.

"Not counting the exit," Gabrielle agreed with a nod.

"Okay," Hamish said, "if that's the low end, what would the high end be, do you think?"

The question hung over them like a cloud, but all eyes turned toward Simon, who admitted, "Some have never been cracked."

"Well, if Hazel *used* the secret compartment, that means she *found* the secret compartment," Kat said, reassuring everyone, but mostly herself. "And if Hazel found it, I'm willing to bet I can too. I just hope it doesn't take too long."

"I'll rig you up with a button cam," Simon told her. "We'll all be able to see what you're seeing, and help if we can."

"Good," Kat said. She was under the distinct impression that she was going to need all the help she could get.

"Are you sure Marianne doesn't know how it works?" Gabrielle asked.

"She swears she doesn't," Kat said. "So that means . . ."

"It might take all night," Simon finished.

"So all night you shall have!" Angus said with a slap of his thigh. Then he scooted close to Simon and whispered, "How do we get her all night?"

Sweat was beading on Simon's brow. "I don't know. No one's ever done the Basil E. Frankweiler at the Henley."

"It'll have to be someplace the guards won't check and the cameras won't see," Gabrielle said. "Simon, can you arrange that?"

"No go," Simon said with a shake of his head.

"You were able to loop the video feeds before," Gabrielle said.

"Yes, but before, the Henley had a chink in their armor. They've fixed it."

Angus opened his mouth to protest, but Simon cut him off.

"Look, we can blind some of the cameras, but it will have to be manual. And temporary. There's no way I can access their system again. Well, no way to easily access their system on this kind of time frame. We're definitely going to need a blind spot."

"So we just have to find a place with no guards and no cameras for eight to twelve hours in the most heavily monitored museum in the world." Kat took a deep breath. "Okay. How hard can that be?"

No one answered, and Kat was glad for the silence. It was times like this when she was supposed to be able to ask her father for advice, her uncle. Her mother. But the truth of the matter was, it was the Henley; and she was the only person she knew who had ever been in and out . . . clean.

Well, almost the only person, Kat realized as another thought occurred to her. "I know what we need."

"What?" Angus asked.

Gabrielle met her cousin's eyes, and finished. "Help."

4 DAYS AFTER
THE READING
OF THE WILL

BRUSSELS,
BELGIUM

CHAPTER 13

In a continent of beautiful places, there was always something Kat liked about Brussels. The Royal Palace. The river Senne. Cathedrals and ancient buildings as far as the eye could see. So she sat on a bench and sipped her coffee, waiting until the church bells chimed three o'clock.

Kat could imagine those big gears turning, moving the hands of the clock and then setting off a chain reaction down the street and across the city, all the way to the halls of St. Christopher's Academy. By the time the bells had finished, the big double doors were swinging open and a tide of blue blazers and book bags emerged. But Kat stayed on her bench, watching, waiting, until one boy appeared among the masses.

He walked with more purpose than his classmates, stood a little straighter. And when he saw her, he didn't even break stride.

"Why do I get the feeling you didn't come all the way to Belgium for an education?" Nick pulled the straps of his backpack over his shoulders and squinted against the sun that reflected off the gold buttons on his private-school blazer.

"Oh, I'm definitely here to learn." Kat couldn't help but smirk as she stood and sidled closer.

"I'm sure you are." Nick gave a wry laugh. "Do I have to ask how you found me?"

"This is the best international school in Brussels—all the European Union bigwigs send their kids here. Congratulations on your mom's promotion, by the way. Interpol Liaison to the EU, very fancy."

"Thanks," he said. "Of course she hates it. Too desk-job-y."

"I'll tell my dad. I'm sure he'll send his condolences."

"I'm sure he will."

Kat had to wonder for a minute what that would feel like—homework and uniforms, walks home with nice boys offering to carry your bag. That was her life once. Almost. But Hale had gotten her kicked out of the Colgan School, pulled her back into her own world, just like now he'd been pulled back into his.

"So why are you here, Kat?" Nick asked.

"Maybe I was craving waffles."

"Kat . . ." He let her name draw out. "I'm pretty sure this is the part where you tell me you need my help to steal an emerald." He laughed. "Or rob the Henley . . ."

Kat's face stayed blank, but something in her eyes must have shifted, because Nick tensed.

"No." It was like he'd read her mind, because he was already shaking his head, saying, "No. No. No. Just—"

"Hear me out, Nick."

She touched his arm, but he jerked away. "Are you crazy?" he said. "No. Strike that. I know you're crazy, but I didn't know you had a death wish."

"It's not what it sounds like."

"It never is with you, is it? And that's the problem."

"That's hilarious coming from you." Kat rolled her eyes. "I remember a time when you couldn't wait to rob the Henley with me. Don't you? Maybe I should ask your mother about it."

"That's probably not a good idea, Kat. She might be too busy trying to arrest your father."

Kat started to fire back, but then stopped. Her breath slowed and she looked up at him. "Why are we fighting?"

He laughed a little. "I honestly have no idea."

"Okay," she said. "As long as I'm not the only one."

They walked together down the cobblestone street, silent for a while until Kat said, "So, school, huh?"

"You know, these days a lot of teenagers are experimenting with formal education."

"It's a regular epidemic."

Nick gave a slow, wide grin. "That's kind of the idea." He shoved his hands into his pockets and kept walking. "So, where is he?"

Kat stopped cold on the street, and Nick guessed the truth.

"Wait. Are you telling me that you intend to rob the Henley—*again*—without Hale?" He sounded both confused and impressed.

"I'm doing it *for* Hale."

Nick laughed. "You mean there's something at the Henley W. W. Hale the Fifth can't buy?"

"It's complicated."

"What else is new?" He looked off into the distance. "What do you need?"

"A blind spot. And someplace with no guard access overnight."

"The Basil E. Frankweiler?" he asked with a grin. "Oh, Kat. You are the craziest genius I know."

"I'll take that as a compliment. Now, will you help me?"

"I would if I could, but my mom is a glorified bureaucrat now. She wouldn't have that kind of information."

"Come on, Nick. You and I both know that all the world's museums keep their security specs on file with Interpol."

"And Kat, you and I both know we're not *at* Interpol."

"You mean to tell me the official Interpol Liaison to the European Union doesn't have database access?"

He couldn't tell her that, and she knew it. So Nick shifted his backpack and started down the sidewalk. "I'll see what I can do."

The airport outside of Brussels was busy, but not busy enough, in Kat's opinion. She kept her bag on her lap and her gaze on the tarmac. At the other end of the terminal a flight was being boarded for New York, and Kat was half tempted to catch it— to run all the way back if she had to, and beg Hale to forgive her; but forgive her for what, she didn't exactly know.

"Mademoiselle McMurray," the gate agent said, but Kat didn't look up. Heavy gray clouds gathered outside, and Kat was trying not to think about the turbulence; her stomach was already lurching up and down. She'd felt queasy for days.

"Mademoiselle?" the woman said again, and Kat suddenly remembered that *McMurray* was the name on her passport.

"We're boarding." The woman spoke English with a heavy French accent.

"*Merci,*" Kat told her, then picked up her bag, handed over her ticket, and joined the long line of passengers crossing through the glass doors and heading toward the plane.

As soon as she stepped outside, the damp breeze hit Kat like a slap. Mist was heavy in the air, and she could feel her short black hair beginning to frizz as it blew across her face, clinging to her cheeks. For a second, Kat thought the wind was howling, that her mind was playing tricks on her when she heard somebody yell, "Kat! Wait!"

The rain was growing heavy, and Kat could see nothing but a dark shadow running from the airport doors toward her. "Hale?" Kat asked. But no. The shape was wrong. The voice was off.

"Wait!" Nick yelled. He was almost panting when he came to a stop beside her. "Hey."

"Hey, yourself," Kat told him.

"I'm glad I caught you. I didn't want you to leave before I could give you your present." He held up a long plastic tube sealed at each end, and Kat's stomach flipped again.

"Is that . . ."

"Complete blueprints for the Henley?" he asked with a wink. "Oh, yeah."

"Hard copies, Nick? How old-fashioned."

"I'm an old-fashioned kind of guy."

And then Kat couldn't joke anymore. She was all out of *tease* when she said, "Thanks, Nick. For this. I owe you."

"I'm not sure *you* do."

"Okay. Hale owes you. I'll take good care of them for—"

Kat reached for the tube, but Nick pulled the blueprints

out of her grasp. "Not so fast. I'm coming with them."

He flashed a boarding pass of his own, Brussels to London one-way.

"You don't have to do that, Nick. I know you've got school and stuff," Kat said. "We'll be fine without—"

"Oh, I'm not doing this for you. I'm doing this so that *these* never have a chance to get back to your uncle. Or your father. I'm sentimental, Kat, not suicidal." He eyed her. "Do you have a problem with that?"

"I have problems, Nick. But you aren't one of them." She headed for the plane and yelled over her shoulder, "Come on."

CHAPTER 14

"**D**oes anyone have any questions?"

Kat sat at the front of the room, the complete blueprints of the Henley taped to the windows, standing between her and that million-dollar view. The lights of London bled through the thin paper, and it was like the documents were on fire. Kat only wished they didn't feel quite so radioactive.

"Are you sure we can't take those off your hands when we're finished, Nick my boy?" Hamish asked with a nod.

Nick crossed his arms. "I'm sure."

"But—" Angus started, but Kat cut him off.

"Guys, Nick didn't have to do this. For us. Or for Hale." She thought for a second about the animosity that had always coursed between the two of them, but didn't linger on the question of why Nick had come. She was simply glad he had.

"In short," she went on, "we owe him."

"Hear, hear." Hamish raised a glass of something they had found in Carlos's refrigerator. "To Nick! And his very hot mum!"

"Thanks," Nick said, but he didn't sound like he meant it.

"So if there aren't any questions . . ." Kat let the words draw out. She scanned the room, looking at the eager faces staring back at her. They would have done anything—gone anywhere—for her or for Hale. She felt a little dizzy with the knowledge that so much was riding on her not making any mistakes.

"Okay. Then I guess we're good."

They all got up to go, but Kat didn't move. She just sat, staring.

"What's the matter, Kitty?" Gabrielle threw open the door to the big Sub-Zero fridge and peered inside. "Cat got your tongue?"

Kat didn't say a thing.

"If you're worried about the timing . . ."

"Are we doing the right thing, Gabrielle?" Kat blurted, finally finding the words she hadn't had the courage to say.

"Personally, I think the Wind in the Willows is a little dated, but if Simon says the cameras are—"

"Not the job. Is this . . . are we doing the right thing?"

"You've got to tell him." Gabrielle's tone was pointed, and Kat didn't ask who "he" was. She didn't have to.

She just looked down at the hardwood floor and said, "I know."

"It's his family, and he has the right to know."

"I know," Kat said again.

"So why *haven't* you told him?"

"I don't know, okay? The reading of the will was so crazy, and then I was going to . . . *I was*," she said again, stronger, when Gabrielle gave her a skeptical look. "But what if Marcus is wrong?"

"He's not," Gabrielle said, certain.

"What if he is, Gabrielle? You didn't see Hale. You didn't hear him. His grandmother is the only person in his family he has ever cared about, and now she's gone, but he's got her company. So it's like he's got a piece of her. If we're right about this . . . If we're right, it's going to be like losing her all over again."

"So it's better to let him go into this—whatever it is— blind? It's better to let him be somebody's mark?"

Kat knew it was her turn to speak—to say something to prove her cousin wrong. But the words didn't come, and Kat just sat there.

"He deserves to know," Gabrielle said again.

"You're right. He does. But something about this . . . scares me."

Gabrielle stepped back and crossed her arms, surveyed her cousin carefully. "Are you scared, or are you angry?"

"Why would I be angry?"

"Come on, Kitty Kat . . ." Gabrielle cocked her head. "You're Hale's secret girlfriend."

"His what?"

"You know, the girl he likes just as long as no one knows it."

"Everyone knows it."

"No." Gabrielle spun on her. "Everyone *you know* knows it. But I'm willing to bet he conveniently forgot to mention the G-word when you met his mother. What about his dad?"

Gabrielle added. "And Little Miss Redhead? What's her name?"

"Natalie," Kat said.

"Yeah." Gabrielle huffed. "I'm sure he was all lovey-dovey in front of her?"

Kat said nothing, and her cousin talked on.

"I'm just saying, if you're sneaking around behind his back because you think something's wrong, fine."

"Of course I think something's wrong."

Gabrielle sidled closer. "But if you're doing it because you *want* something to be wrong . . ."

"What do you mean?"

"I mean the owner of Hale Industries might not be able to go to Rome to steal a Rembrandt on a whim. I mean, maybe a guy who is concerned with stock prices might forget to care about long cons." Gabrielle sidled even closer, hand on hip. "What I mean, dear cousin, is that maybe you want Hale to get out of *his* family's business because that is the only way to keep him in *yours*."

It was more than a little embarrassing how much time Kat spent wishing her cousin were wrong but knowing in her heart she wasn't. It wasn't fair that Gabrielle could be both so beautiful and so wise.

"Get some sleep, Kitty Kat." Gabrielle started up the stairs. "You're spending tomorrow night at the museum."

5 DAYS AFTER
THE READING
OF THE WILL

LONDON,
ENGLAND

CHAPTER 15

The good news, Kat couldn't help but think, was that the Petrovich exhibit was far from the most impressive thing among the Henley's always impressive collection. Sitting as it was, in the center of the grand promenade, it was easy for the guards and the docents and even the visitors themselves to overlook it, to treat the dozen prominent pieces less like valuable works of art and more like . . . well . . . furniture.

Desks and bookcases and even chests of drawers filled the center of the corridor with only red velvet ropes standing between the precious works and the sticky hands of sweaty tourists.

The crowds were heavy and the winds outside were brisk, so even Kat had to concede that the conditions were as perfect as they could be, given the circumstances. But the circumstances, any decent thief would know, were far from good.

It was still the Henley, and Kat and her crew were still the kids who'd robbed it, and so it was with more than a little trepidation that she followed Gabrielle (who had been forced to abandon her short skirts and tall heels for the occasion, lest any of the guards recollected seeing her legs on that fateful day last December).

The past was the past, and the people at the Henley seemed to go about their business as if nothing at all had changed.

Kat, on the other hand, knew better.

The guards were on a different rotation. The cameras had been upgraded no more than a month before. The security system was running on an entirely different feed, and this time Kat could see Simon out of the corner of her eye, lingering by the doors to the North Garden. His hands were shaking as he paced back and forth, looking like he was going to burst through the doors and run screaming from the Henley at any moment. But he didn't.

"I don't like this. I feel naked. I feel . . . blind," Simon said through the comms unit.

"Then push your wig back," Gabrielle told him from her place by the windows.

But that wasn't the problem, and Kat knew it.

"It's no fair," Simon said. "They get to have computers. And cameras. With facial-recognition software. Have I mentioned I am *not* a fan of facial-recognition software?"

"Yeah," Gabrielle told him. "You might have mentioned it when you were shopping for fake noses."

Simon defended his honor. Gabrielle insulted his nose. But the words were just a distant humming in Kat's ears as she walked down the long main corridor filled with desks and cabinets, a bookcase from the library of a very famous university that had been transplanted there piece by piece, including the very secret compartment behind it.

Kat moved slowly, taking it all in.

And then she saw it—the desk in the middle of the exhibit—twenty yards from the entrance to the Imperial China room, directly opposite the portrait of Veronica Henley herself. Kat thought of another fine old lady as she inched closer to the velvet ropes.

It wasn't the most ornate of the pieces, but it was Kat's favorite—the very one she would have chosen if she could have picked any Petrovich for herself. The drawers were intricately carved. The pass-through underneath had a swinging door. The top was soft leather with small brass studs. It was masculine, Kat thought; not the place for an old woman's thank-you notes and diaries. No. It was a desk made for business, and Kat imagined Hazel there, filling her husband's seat quite literally as she carried both the family and the company into a new era.

"I still wish I had a computer," Simon said from his place by the doors.

Kat pulled her thoughts and her gaze away from Hazel's desk and studied the long corridor.

"We don't need a computer, Simon," Kat said. "We just need them."

To any casual observer, she was probably pointing at the herd of schoolchildren that was walking down the promenade and toward the main doors. It was easy to miss Nick, who lingered at the far end of the hall, and the Bagshaws, who were walking in her direction, a tall, steaming cup of coffee in Angus's hands.

"Attention Henley guests," a woman's voice announced over the loudspeakers, "we have reached our close of business. Please make your way to the doors, and remember, the museum will open again at nine a.m. tomorrow morning. Thank you for visiting the Henley, and have a lovely evening."

The schoolchildren walked a little faster. The docents gestured the crowd toward the doors. And, quietly, Kat said, "Now."

Though the management of the Henley would never say so aloud, no one was really certain what had happened that afternoon. Of the two dozen school groups that had been scheduled to visit, not a single teacher seemed to know where the children got the items they eventually carried through the Henley's halls. A staffer had handed them out, somebody said. It was some kind of free promotion gone wrong, others assumed.

But the truth remained that of the hundred children who walked through the Henley at the close of business on that particular day, approximately half of them were carrying helium-filled balloons in a variety of colors. The other half had small whirligigs, the kind depicted in a sculpture by a new Swiss artist of much acclaim.

And absolutely no one knew exactly how or why the doors at either end of the long hallway opened at the same time, sending a massive gush of wind rushing through the Henley.

The small toys began to spin. Wild splashes of color and flashes of light filled the corridor. Balloons flew free of their owners' hands, blinding the cameras and popping against the hot lights overhead. The noise must have been in the same frequency as breaking glass, because the sensors in the control room went haywire. And even the Henley guards, with their highly expert surveillance videos, could see nothing beyond the glare.

They didn't even notice when a very tall, very hot cup of coffee went flying over the velvet ropes and landed on the leather-covered desktop that had once belonged to the Hale family's London estate.

And when the chaos finally ended, all that remained were broken balloons and a stained desk, and the security experts who agreed that things could have been far, far worse.

Workmen appeared.

Dollies were ordered.

But no one noticed that the desk was heavier than it had been when they'd moved it onto the exhibit floor only a few days before.

They never even looked in the small pass-through compartment, where Katarina Bishop hid, clinging for dear life.

CHAPTER 16

Kat was beginning to think that Simon was right: it was absolutely no fun being blind. But true to her name, her eyes adjusted to the black as she stayed perfectly still in her hiding spot beneath the desk.

If Nick and his blueprints were accurate, there was one room where there were no cameras. In the center of the basement, with no exterior access of any kind, there was one place where no guards would ever have to patrol. So Kat stayed hidden, and when the desk stopped moving, she listened as the sound of work boots on concrete faded in the distance. And once certain she was alone, she dropped to the floor, rolled out from under the desk, and surveyed the dim and empty room.

There were tall shelves with jars of varnish and paint in

every shade, long tables lined with tools and brushes. It was a place where meticulous people did meticulous work, and part of Kat couldn't help being impressed.

She stepped around the room, studying the works in progress. There was a pair of portraits by Matisse, a sculpture by Rodin. The piece of DNA she shared with Uncle Eddie tugged at her, and her mind flashed with exit strategies and all the ways that one might carry a twelve-hundred-pound Greek relic out of the fifth-most secure building in Britain. But then the beam of her favorite flashlight shone across the ornate desk, and Kat knew what she had to do.

There, without the velvet rope, Kat was free to feel the intricate carvings. She ran her fingers over acorns and trees, bows and arrows. Kat examined every inch. It was exquisite. But there was one part that seemed wrong. On each of the desk's four corners there were markings, like needles of a compass, and one of them pointed in the wrong direction.

"Well, hello there," Kat said. "What do you do?"

As soon as Kat turned the arrow, she heard the tiniest of clicks.

"I got it," she whispered. "Did I get it?" she asked, then looked to see a narrow piece of the baseboard that had popped free from the rest of the desk. She sank to her knees and shined her light inside, stuck a hand into the dusty space until she felt a single piece of paper.

But wait. It wasn't paper. Not really. Kat held it against the light. It was carbon paper, black with faint white letters—the kind offices used to make duplicates of important documents in the days before computers and even copy machines. The carbon had probably been in the desk for years. And it was only one page—

"It's not here," Kat said, defeated. She crumbled the carbon and put it into her pocket.

"Wait, Kat." Simon's voice was in her ear. "Petrovich didn't put just one compartment in his pieces. There would be two or three at least. Keep on looking."

"It's okay, Kat," Nick said. "You have all the time you need."

So Kat went back to work. She opened drawers and felt inside shelves. She ran her delicate fingers beneath the lip of the desktop and along all four legs. There was a nick on the top right-hand corner, but it was just a flaw, Kat realized—not a clue.

She had all night, Kat had to remind herself. Come morning, she could slip outside and into the crowds that filled the Henley. All she had to do was think and feel and see.

So Kat stepped away from the desk, walked to the far corner of the room, and studied not the carvings but the desk as a whole. It was gorgeous. At least three different kinds of wood had been used, and they blended together beautifully. Seamlessly. Alternating one with the next. It was almost like . . .

"A chessboard," she whispered, the words only for herself.

Carefully, Kat circled the desk, eyeing it from every angle.

"Uh . . ." Hamish said through the comms unit. "You know how no one was supposed to realize who spilled the drink?"

"Yeah?" Gabrielle sounded worried, but Kat kept her gaze locked on the desk, walking around and around.

"I think they figured it out!" Angus yelled. "Run!"

Somewhere on the grounds of the Henley, the Bagshaws were making a break for it, but Kat never took her eyes off the desk.

There were so many intricate pieces. They had to fit together somehow, Kat was certain. She walked to the front of the desk again, pushed against one of the panels, but nothing moved. She repeated the gesture on every square, but they were all firm and solid. She was about to give up when her fingers traced over something that felt different.

Kat leaned down and shined her light onto the small square. The difference in the coloring was so minuscule, she doubted anyone would ever notice; but the feel was off, somehow. Kat took her fingernail and scraped against the priceless desk, and a small amount of a very soft substance rubbed away. Restorer's putty, Kat knew. Something was there—some blemish or flaw that had been covered over within the past week.

Kat found that place, pressed again, twisted; and from somewhere deep inside the desk, she heard a tiny click.

"Hamish, don't go down the alley!" Gabrielle yelled through her comms unit, but that wasn't the reason Kat's pulse was racing as she walked to the back of the desk, looking for any other moving pieces.

"Kat," Simon said, but Kat barely heard him. She might have been looking at a desk, but what she saw were patterns and pictures, a map through the maze.

"Kat!" Simon shouted in her ear. She was about to lash out that she was busy when he whispered, "Hide."

Before Kat could ask what he meant, there was a slice of light across the concrete, and Kat's mouth went wide with shock. She darted from the desk, crouching low and diving behind the tall shelves that filled the center of the room. She felt her flashlight slip from her hand and go skidding across the concrete floor, but she couldn't chase it. She could do nothing but stay low, hidden in the shadows, while three men walked toward her.

"There's a light switch around here. . . . Yes. There," a man said, and a moment later the overhead fluorescents flickered to life.

It took all of Kat's willpower not to gasp when she heard a familiar voice saying, "Now, perhaps you can tell us what you meant—the Hale desk was involved in an accident?"

"Yes, Mr. Garrett. As I was trying to tell you earlier, it's nothing, really. Our restoration department is the finest in the world, more than capable of mopping up a little spill. I assure you, Mr. Hale, you have nothing to worry about."

Mr. Hale.

Kat peeked through the crack in the shelves, and what she saw was broad shoulders and a charismatic smile. But there was something infinitely sad about the boy in the very nice suit who stood with two men, staring down at the desk.

"I guarantee you . . . sir," the stranger said, "your late grandfather's desk is—"

"Grandmother's."

"Pardon?" the director asked.

"My great-great-great-grandfather purchased this desk, but it was my late grandmother who truly owned it."

"I see," the man said with a solemn nod.

"Where's that artist, Duncan?" Garrett asked, and the director began to squirm.

"I'm sure she'll be right along."

"You're the director of this facility. Go find her," Garrett snapped.

"Of course, sir. Right away."

Kat watched in silence as the man from the museum scurried through the swinging doors, leaving Hale and Garrett alone among the paint and the brushes.

"Why are we here?" Hale sounded like he was mid-con and playing a bored and elusive billionaire. Then Kat had to remind herself he wasn't playing.

"I told you, Scooter. Hale Industries has a significant presence in Europe. It's important for you to at least put in an appearance at the London headquarters."

"No." Hale took a deep breath. "Why are we *here*?" He held out his arms and gestured at the walls and shelves covered with priceless paintings and delicate sculptures. He sat on a workbench as the man looked down on him and gave a condescending smile.

"Well, it's the finest museum in the world."

"I know."

"Oh, I know you do," Garrett said, and for a split second, Kat wondered exactly what he was saying. She watched Hale, but the words didn't seem to register with him.

"You're an important man now, Scooter. You have responsibilities."

"Isn't that why I have you?"

"Well, yes." Garrett laughed a little. "I guess it is."

Hale stood and reached for the desk, ran his hand along the small section that Kat had been examining only moments before.

"What is it?" Garrett asked.

"I did that," Hale said, pointing to the flaw that had been filled with putty.

"You carved into an original Petrovich?"

107

"Hazel told me to," Hale countered. "I was . . . I don't know . . . six or seven and she gave me a knife—told me that that was where *H* would mark the spot."

For a moment, Hale's trustee was quiet. Then he jerked his head toward the door. "Why don't you go check on Duncan, Scooter? Make sure he brings that woman back. This is your grandmother's desk. We can't have it damaged further."

When Hale left, Kat felt frozen, watching as Garrett walked around the desk, studying the ornate carvings. She couldn't breathe as the man turned the piece of the desk where Hale had pointed. A small hidden drawer opened with an ominous pop. To Kat, it sounded like a bubble bursting as a narrow piece of molding slid away from the rest of the desk, and the man reached inside and pulled out a pile of papers held together by a single clip. Quickly, he slipped them into an interior pocket of his suit coat.

"He's got it," Kat said.

"What?" Gabrielle asked. "No, Angus, you need to get out of the garden! I'm sorry, Kat. What were you—"

"He's got it. Garrett has the will." The words were almost for herself, because, in that moment, the girl who always had a plan had absolutely no idea what to do. Options and alternatives swirled in her mind, but before she could do a single thing, Director Duncan appeared at the doorway, Hale at his side.

"She's on her way, Mr. Garrett," the director said, but Garrett no longer seemed interested.

Instead, he spoke directly to the boy. "Come, Scooter, we've seen enough. We'll get out of your way, Mr. Duncan."

"But . . ." The director seemed befuddled.

"You're a busy man, and we're jet-lagged. Come on, Scooter, let's go."

Two guards appeared and asked the director a question, so Kat kept herself pressed against the wall and whispered as loudly as she dared, "Gabrielle, Simon?"

"I'm here, Kat." The voice was Nick's.

"Garrett's leaving with the real will. We've got to get it back. Now!"

CHAPTER 17

There are moments in any thief's career that seem to last a lifetime—the second it takes for a guard to check a window, for the security camera to sweep. But the longest minute that Kat Bishop ever lived through was the one that came after she saw Hale and his trustee disappear through the door of the Henley's restoration room. She could hear the museum director chatting with the guards on the other side of the shelves. Her crew was shouting out orders and questions, rapid-fire in her ear. But Kat could do nothing but stand and wait and listen.

"I have them at the north entrance," Gabrielle said.

"Hamish, Angus, you clear?" Nick asked.

"As a bell, Nicky boy," Hamish said.

"Kat, what are you going to do?" Simon asked. "Kat?"

The comms unit squeaked—an almost deafening sound—and Kat threw her hand to her ear, trying to keep it in.

"What was that?" a guard asked.

There were footsteps on the concrete, and Kat pressed herself more tightly against the shelves.

"There," the director said. "Look at that."

Kat held her breath. She closed her eyes.

"Just look at those rubbish bins. When was the last time they were emptied?" The director sounded mortified and ashamed. "You lads notify the janitorial staff. I want a full crew down here now."

She heard the door open and close, and for a second, Kat was alone.

"Garrett," Kat whispered. "Stick with Garrett. I'll be right there."

"Kat, no!" Nick shouted. "You can't get out of there unseen until the morning. It's too risky."

But Kat just smiled. "I'll see you soon."

On the streets near the Henley that day, there were any number of odd things that could have easily been seen by anyone who cared to look.

First, there was a pair of ruddy-faced boys who were scaling the fence that surrounded the gardens. Two guards were in hot pursuit, but no one bothered to summon Scotland Yard or even the police. And once the boys had run into the nearest Tube station, the guards, huffing and puffing, gave up their chase and went back inside.

The second fairly strange thing was that a long black limousine was sitting at the opposite side of the building. It wasn't parked. It did not circle. Instead, the car just idled by the main entrance as if, at any moment, a very well-financed thief was going to stroll out the front doors of the Henley and make an incredibly elegant escape. But anyone expecting that scenario would have been disappointed when a boy emerged through the Henley's doors, an older man at his side.

The man hurried away from the museum, throwing cautious looks over his shoulder. But the boy walked into the fleeting sunlight as if there were no place on earth where he would not feel at ease.

The pair was almost to the limousine when the man said something, and a moment later, the boy climbed into the backseat alone. When the limo drove off, the man continued on foot, disappearing into the crowded streets. He seemed perfectly unaware when yet another boy emerged from the Henley's doors with the last few straggling visitors of the day. This boy wore dark glasses and kept an even, steady pace, always fifty feet or so at the man's back.

But the oddest sight of all came when the janitorial staff carried the day's rubbish to the large bins in the back of the building. The men chatted as they dumped the cans into the massive dumpster, straining a bit under their weight before going back inside.

Not one of them saw the girl who emerged from the dumpster a minute later, filthy and disheveled. She dropped to the ground and ran.

"Where is he?" Kat asked as she bolted down the street.

"We're almost to the Thames."

"Stay with him, Nick," Kat said.

"Don't worry. He's not going anywhere."

"Hamish? Angus?" Kat asked. "Help Nick."

"On it, Kitty," Hamish answered back.

Kat heard a roar behind her and turned just in time to see Gabrielle on a motorcycle, speeding her way.

Gabrielle pulled to the side of the street and yelled, "Get on!" but Kat wasn't waiting for an invitation.

"I think this might be my first high-speed chase," Simon said from the sidecar. Gabrielle banked hard, careening around a curve. "I'm not sure I like it!"

"Nick, where is he?" Kat asked, but was met with only silence. Gabrielle revved the bike and Kat asked again, "Nick? Angus? Hamish?"

"Our comms units are running out of a van in the Henley parking lot," Simon said. "We must be out of range."

As they neared the Tower of London, the traffic began to congest and clog, tour buses and red double-deckers merging with black cabs and service vans, all full of people trying to fight their way across the river.

But there was only one face that mattered, so Kat put her hands on Gabrielle's shoulders and stood, scanning the crowds that filled the busy street.

"Kat." Nick's voice came through her earpiece. It was scratchy and garbled and Kat only made out one word. ". . . bridge . . ."

That was all she needed to hear. In a flash, Kat was off the bike and running past the House of Parliament, through the shadow of Big Ben.

"Kat, what do you want us to do?" Nick finally said, his voice clear. "Kat, do you want us to approach him?"

She could see Nick near the Bagshaws fifty feet away from Garrett on the opposite side of the street. They stood shielded by the traffic and pedestrians, lingering with the vendors and artists who gathered, hocking their wares to the tourists.

But one man wasn't there for the sights. Kat was on the bridge, pushing through the crowds, when she saw him stop at the rail and reach into his pocket. A second later, the papers were in his hands.

"Kat?" Nick asked.

"Stop him," Kat said, but the static must have come again, they were so far from Simon's base at the Henley. "Stop him!" she shouted, but it was too late. The boys couldn't see when the man pulled a lighter from his pocket. No one noticed a thing until flames began to lick at the corners of the pages, and soon they were alive with fire, crumbling into black and falling into the Thames.

CHAPTER 18

Katarina Bishop was not a girl unaccustomed to setbacks. She'd been born into a world of Plan A, B, C, and at the very least, D. She knew things never went exactly according to plan, but never before had she been so clueless about what could or should come next.

She could call Eddie and ask for advice, but Eddie had a strict "Do Not Disturb Unless Someone Is Bleeding" policy. She could go to her father, but she wasn't exactly sure where he was or if he'd forgive her when he found out she'd had the complete blueprints to the Henley and had only tried to steal a stack of papers.

Nick and his blueprints were on a flight back to Brussels and his mom and his school. He'd done all he could to help, and now the only thing Kat knew for certain was that Hale's world was different from hers. They spoke a different language, played by different rules. So as she walked into Carlos's apartment an hour later, Kat couldn't shake the feeling that the only person who could help was the only person she absolutely couldn't call.

Then a ray of light came slicing through the dark. Literally. Kat threw her hands up to shield against it, and Angus and Hamish bolted toward the outline of a man in a chair. They were almost there when Gabrielle reached for the switch on the wall and the kitchen lights flickered on, freezing Kat and her crew where they stood.

"You dropped this." Hale turned off the flashlight that Kat had last seen skidding across the Henley's concrete floor. "Thought you might want it back."

"Thanks," she said. "It's my favorite."

"I know."

"How'd you find us?" Kat asked.

"I met this girl once. . . . She taught me all kinds of useful things."

"She sounds like a keeper," Kat said, but this time Hale made no reply.

Instead, he stood and examined the large room. "So, this is a nice place."

"It belongs to Carlos," Angus said.

"Carlos is Cuban," Hamish finished.

"Good for him," Hale said. And then he stopped. There were four other people in the room, but Hale only looked at Kat, and something in his gaze burned her, froze her, made her want to run.

"I can explain," she blurted.

"I'm sure you can. But I don't want an explanation, Katarina. I'd rather have the truth." The playful smile was gone. The spark in his eyes was extinguished. There was nothing but cold fury that stared back at her when he asked, "Why are you in London, Kat?"

"I tried to tell you, Hale, but—"

He took a slow step closer. "Why are you in London?"

"It's probably nothing. And I didn't want to worry you until we knew something for sure, so—"

"Why. Are. You. In. London?"

"Hale . . ." Kat reached for his hand, but he pulled away. He couldn't touch her. "We came to get something out of your grandmother's desk."

"What?" he asked.

"We think . . . we heard that she might have had a different will. And we came to see for ourselves."

"That's ridiculous." Hale shook his head. "Why would you think such a thing?"

For the first time, from the corner of Kat's eye, she saw Marcus. He stood stoically at attention as always, but right then he made a subtle shift. He opened his mouth to speak, but before he could say a word, Kat said, "Uncle Eddie."

"What about him?" Hale asked.

"He heard the will was a fake," Gabrielle said. "A really good con."

"So Uncle Eddie heard that my grandmother's will was a fake?" Hale asked. "But you don't come to me. You don't say a thing to me because . . . Why didn't you say anything, Kat? Why would you . . ." Then Hale's voice trailed off. He glanced toward the window with its views of the Tower and Buckingham Palace—places of power, family. Deceit. And his voice was cold when he said, "I'm not really the heir, am I?"

Of all the lies Kat had told in her life, not one was harder than the truth.

"I don't know. But something's wrong, Hale. We don't know what, exactly, but your grandmother did leave some papers in that desk."

Hale spun on her. "What did they say?"

Kat hung her head. "Garrett got to them before I did. They're gone, Hale. I'm sorry."

"What did they say?" he asked, his voice cold.

"We don't know," Gabrielle said. But Hale just kept looking at Kat. "Sure you do. Don't you, Kat?"

"It might have been a will. I don't know, though. Like I said, Garrett got to the papers first. And then he destroyed them. They're gone, Hale. I'm sorry. I'm so—"

"So you think Garrett's behind all of this? So he can . . . what? What's his endgame? What does he want?" Hale sounded very much like someone trying to look at things objectively. As though it were just another job.

Kat shrugged. "We don't have a clue."

"You know who might have been able to help with that?" Hale shouted. "Me!"

"Hale," Kat said, reaching for him; but he pulled away. "I wanted to tell you, but—"

"But what, Kat? But I couldn't be trusted? But I'm too immature to keep a secret? Maybe you think I'm a screw-up, too."

"That's not it."

"Then what *is* it?"

"I saw him destroy those papers, Hale," Kat countered.

"Yeah. Exactly. Papers. They could have been anything. This proves nothing." He stormed toward the door, then stopped short. "No. Wait. It proves I don't have a girlfriend anymore."

6 DAYS AFTER
THE READING
OF THE WILL

BROOKLYN, NEW YORK,
USA

CHAPTER 19

Sleep every chance you get. Eat every chance you get. These were two of many lessons that Kat had learned at her father's knee and her uncle's table, but on the long flight over the Atlantic, she couldn't manage to doze. She wanted to blame it on her coach-class ticket, but every time she closed her eyes, she heard Hale's words and the slamming door. It felt like a dream on a constant loop inside her head, and as much as she wanted to press pause, it just kept playing over and over, and the scene never changed.

Not on the walk through the airport. Not during the long ride in the back of the cab. Even standing on Uncle Eddie's stoop, Kat still saw the look on Hale's face, and for once she had absolutely no idea how to steal the thing she really wanted.

"Don't worry," Gabrielle said. "He'll get over it."

Kat put her key in the lock and looked out over the sleepy street. Newspapers lay waiting for owners; the bakery on the corner had hot bagels and warm coffee. Gabrielle gave a full-body stretch and never once complained about the discomfort of the flight. There are some things even worse than flying coach internationally, and Gab knew it.

"He'll come around," she said. "Trust me, boys always come around."

But that wasn't it, so Kat shifted. "I'm not worried. I'm scared."

"Hale will be fine. He's just got to—"

"Not about Hale. Garrett. There was this moment in London . . . It was like . . ." She trailed off, unable to say the words aloud.

"What?"

"It was almost like he knew I was there. Or he was expecting me to be there or something."

"You're getting paranoid in your old age," Gabrielle teased, but Kat didn't think it was funny.

"Remember what Marianne said? About Garrett?"

"You mean how she was surprised that Hazel never got around to firing him?"

"Well, looks like that's not exactly correct." Kat handed Gabrielle the piece of carbon paper that she had found in the desk.

"How old is this?" Gabrielle asked with a laugh, but then her eyes scanned over the copy.

"Hazel typed that letter four days before her coma—two days before she arrived in New York."

Gabrielle stopped reading. "So Hazel was old-fashioned? What does that . . ."

"Read the first line. Right there." Kat pointed to the words. "It's a termination letter. Hazel did fire Garrett. And five days later, she died."

Neither Kat nor Gabrielle mentioned those facts again as they let themselves into their uncle's house and made their way toward the kitchen. They didn't reach for a light. They didn't have to. Even without their particular skill sets, the walk was one they both knew well.

"And . . . ?" Eddie said just before they reached the kitchen.

When Gabrielle shook her head, Eddie hung his and gave each niece a pat on the back. "It was a good thing you did for your young man, Katarina."

Kat was fairly certain that Uncle Eddie was the smartest person she'd ever known, but right then she was equally certain he was wrong. He hadn't seen the look in Hale's eyes. He hadn't heard the fury in his voice. Eddie didn't know what Kat had spent the past twelve hours fearing—that she had flown all the way to London only to lose something she could never, ever steal back.

Kat wanted to tell him, beg him to explain to her exactly how she could go back in time and do it all differently. But she didn't bother. Even Uncle Eddie couldn't con the clock.

She just sat quietly as her uncle headed upstairs; but when he reached the door, he gave one last backward wave toward the table.

"Something came for you, Katarina."

There was a letter on the table. As soon as Kat touched it,

she knew it was important. The paper was heavy cotton, and her name was printed on the front in gold embossment. She turned over the envelope and ran her hand along the raised letters that read GENESIS.

Kat took a paring knife and slit the envelope open in one smooth gesture, then pulled out a card and looked down at the words *You are cordially invited to witness the beginning.*

There was the address of Hale Industries and a date and time for the following afternoon. But the thing that made her heart beat faster was the handwritten line at the bottom of the card.

Please come. Use the back door.

"What is it?" her cousin asked.

"I'm not sure," Kat said, turning the card over and over in her hands. "Some kind of invitation."

But to what, she didn't have a clue.

7 DAYS AFTER
THE READING
OF THE WILL

HALE INDUSTRIES
INTERNATIONAL
NEW YORK, NEW YORK,
USA

CHAPTER 20

At half past noon the next day, Kat found herself in the narrow alley behind Hale Industries' world headquarters, staring at a locked door. It seemed utterly wrong to stand at the service entrance with an invitation and not a tool belt, and part of Kat wanted to flee the scene. Run. Disappear into the midtown traffic. But before she could move, a shadow appeared on the wall just over her shoulder, and a vaguely familiar voice said, "Well, hello there."

Kat looked at the man coming up the alley behind her. Immediately, she recognized the white hair and bulging belly. But there was something different about the man whom she'd met at the funeral. This time, he wasn't in mourning. This time, he was . . . nervous.

"Hi, Mr. Foster," Kat said.

Silas nodded, impressed. "That's a good memory you have there."

"Thank you," Kat said. "I try."

"Allow me." Silas swiped his ID badge across an electronic pad beside the door, and Kat gave a soft sigh.

"The McClintock Three-sixty," she whispered when the light flashed from red to green.

"What was that?" he asked.

"That lock is really nifty," Kat hurried to add, then smiled and bounced on the balls of her feet. She must have looked far more innocent than she felt, because the old man opened the door wide and gestured for her to go ahead.

"Come on in," he told her. "I'll show you the way."

Kat had never been inside the Hale Industries headquarters before, but she didn't pause to consider the irony. She was there. Hale had invited her. And the fact that he'd sent her through the back door might not have meant anything at all.

"Come along, Miss Bishop. I believe the party is upstairs."

Mr. Foster pushed the elevator call button, and a moment later, Kat was inside, achingly aware of the silence that filled the shiny car.

"I'm so glad to see you here," Silas told her. "It's a big day for us."

"What *is* today, if you don't mind my asking?"

"Well, before Hazel died, she and I were working on a new project. Today we unveil it for the board of directors. The real party is next week—a *gala*, I believe they're calling it. You should come to that, too. It's going to be quite the big to-do."

"Sounds exciting," Kat said, and laughed a little at the old-fashioned phrase.

"It is," Silas said. "I'm only sad Hazel won't be here to see it."

The elevator made a *ding* and came to a stop.

"Allow me." Silas held open the doors and gestured for Kat to step out into a corridor lined with paintings. There was something eerily familiar about them all, and Kat was just starting to wonder what it was when Silas said, "Miss Bishop, allow me to introduce the Hale men."

He gestured to an old oil painting of a man in uniform. "That's Mr. Hale the First. He was something of a character, I'm told. A big brute of a man. Powerful." Silas puffed up his chest as if to prove the point. "He served in the military with one of the British princes. Saved his life, even, if the stories are true. And was rewarded handsomely for it."

The next painting showed a man on a factory line, surrounded by crates and machinery.

"Mr. Hale the Second," Silas said. "He was the first to come to this country, I believe. A bright man, by all accounts. Greedy. But bright."

They took a few more steps, and Kat came even with two matching portraits.

"W. W. the Third is on your left," Silas said. "And that's his little brother Reginald on the right."

"W. W. the Third was Hazel's husband?" Kat asked.

"He was. He commissioned this building in 1969." Silas smiled a little with the memory, then lowered his voice. "But make no mistake about it, my dear, this is the house that Hazel built."

Silas eased down the long hall, to the last portrait hanging

129

in the row. It was the same image that had run in the paper, and Kat looked at the original, wishing she'd known the woman behind it.

"As much as the Hales understand money, Hazel understood people," Silas said. "None of these old boys would say so, but this place changed when she came on board." He leaned close to Kat and whispered, "For the better."

Kat couldn't pry her gaze away from the portrait. She wished more than anything that she could ask that woman for advice.

"Are you okay, my dear?" Silas Foster asked. Something in the way he looked at her made Kat forget herself for a moment. He seemed so wise and sage and trustworthy, and Kat wanted to tell him everything—about Hazel and Marianne, the will and the trustee's trip to London.

And Hale.

Kat wanted to tell Silas that her boyfriend wasn't her boyfriend anymore, and beg him to go down to his lab and create a device that would make everything okay.

"Kat?" he asked again. "Are you all right?"

"Yes. I'm just a little . . ." Kat began, but she didn't know how to continue. So instead she asked the question that had been on her mind for hours. "Mr. Foster, what *is* Genesis?"

Silas gave a knowing smile. "I guess we're getting ready to find out."

Then she watched the man push open a set of double doors, unsure what she was going to find on the other side, totally not expecting what she saw.

Hale. What Kat saw was Hale.

And he was angry.

Kat knew it the second his gaze met hers. His eyes narrowed and his face flushed. He seemed so much older than sixteen, as though the paintings in the hall had come to life and there he stood—a future tycoon being groomed for greatness. But instead of his father's blank, professional stare, Hale's face was full of rage; and as he headed her way, Kat had every reason to be shaking.

"What are you doing here?"

He was the person she knew best, trusted most, and in spite of all that, she recoiled from his touch. "You invited me," she said.

"No. I *didn't*."

"But . . ." Kat began, then let the words trail off.

"Look, Kat. It's not personal. It's just that this isn't really a public thing."

"I didn't realize I was the public."

"You need to leave, Kat. You just . . ." And then the most naturally gifted inside man that Kat had ever seen was stumbling for words. "I just . . . Who invited you?"

"I did." Kat felt Silas's hand at her back. "Genesis isn't for my generation—it's for yours. Thought it wouldn't hurt to have an extra set of young eyes on it."

"Oh." Hale forced a smile at Silas and then shifted his gaze to Kat. "I see."

Kat wanted to feel her blood boiling, to find the strength to yell, but everything was going cold instead.

"Now, you two have fun." Silas gave them a wink and crossed the room.

Marcus was there, floating through the crowd with a tray of champagne. She recognized several people from the funeral—members of the board, Kat assumed. Hale's mother stood alone in the corner. And something about it all made Kat feel small, inconsequential. Even with Hale beside her, she had never felt more alone in her life.

"Hale, can I talk to you for a second?"

"Son?" Senior was walking toward them, looking right through Kat as if she didn't exist at all.

"I've got to go, Kat," Hale said, but all Kat heard was her cousin's voice whispering the words *secret girlfriend*. . . .

And then a different set of words flashed through her mind: *I don't have a girlfriend anymore*. . . .

"Hale"—she pulled him close—"we need to talk."

But Hale just brushed her aside. "I'm through talking."

Kat didn't want to make a scene—it went against her upbringing, her DNA. So she let him leave. And even though he never looked back, Kat could feel somebody watching, staring.

She turned, taking in the room, and there he was, on the other side of the lab. At least a dozen people stood between them, and yet Kat knew that Garrett was looking right at her. Not blinking. Not smiling.

A good job was nothing more than a play, Kat believed. And right then she couldn't forget that she was backstage at someone else's con. Kat wanted to shout and point at Garrett, tell everyone what he'd done. She felt the words bubbling up inside her, but before they could break free, Silas moved to the center of the room.

"If I can have your attention, please," he called to the men and women assembled. He looked and sounded almost like a preacher when he said, "Thank you for joining us today. As everyone in this room knows, we're here because Hazel wanted a new beginning for Hale Industries. A fresh start. A Genesis, if you will."

Silas walked to a wall safe in the corner of the room. It was an excellent model, and Kat was impressed. She had no idea what kind of scientist the man was, but at least he had good taste in safes.

"Hazel came to this very room several years ago, and together we talked about the future. Of Hale Industries. Of the Hale family. And—not to put too fine a point on it—the world. Hazel knew she wasn't going to live forever—none of us will. But she wanted to build something that would last for generations—something that would alter everything we touch. Something every man and woman could carry in the palm of their hand and be better for it."

When Silas reached into the safe, it was as though the whole room was holding its breath. He held his hands out, like an offering, and then gazed down at the tiny device that lay there.

It was smaller than a deck of cards, gleaming and shining under the bright lights of the lab. When Silas held it up for the audience to see, Kat wasn't exactly sure what she was looking at. But then again, she realized, that was kind of the idea. This was new, fresh. Big. And it was Hale's.

"Genesis, simply put, is power." Silas pointed to the sleek panels that formed the device's shell. "These pull energy from the sun." He slid open a tiny door to reveal the delicate workings inside. "This technology harnesses kinetic energy so that every time the device moves, shakes, tilts—that energy is converted as well."

Silas closed the device and held it aloft again. "All of this technology has existed for years. We just combined it and shrunk it, and now . . . hopefully . . . it is in a package that can change the world."

Silas took a cord from the table and attached one end to the Genesis prototype. Then he picked up a cell phone and removed its battery. "Whatever you need charged—whenever it needs charging—all you have to do is plug Genesis in." He attached the powerless cell phone to the prototype, and instantly the phone sprang to life.

Kat felt the room change. No one moved or spoke for a long time. There was nothing but a long beep and a solemn hush to mark the occasion before, finally, one of the board members dared to speak.

"Foster?" The man cleared his throat. "Are you saying . . . What you mean to tell us is that Genesis *works?*"

"Yes." Silas gave an *I told you so* smirk. "It does. Of course, this is just a prototype—just one model. But given time, I think Hale Industries could use this technology in a way that touches almost everything. Cell phones. Laptops. I suspect even cars could eventually be completely self-sustaining."

Kat looked down at the small device one more time. It felt like all of Hale Industries could fit in the palm of her hand. People crowded around Silas, wanting to see the prototype up close, ask him questions. She could feel the whole tide rising, and she knew that the board was pleased. Hale Industries would be fine. They didn't need Hale, didn't need him at all, so she reached for his hand and pulled him from the crowd.

"Hale, can I talk to you?"

"It's incredible." He looked at her. "Isn't it incredible?"

"Yeah, but that's not why I'm—"

"Hazel should have seen this."

"Hale . . ." Kat said again, but Hale was walking away.

She tried to follow him, but a most unusual roadblock stood in her way.

"Well, hello again," Hale's mother said. She'd traded her black dress for purple, and her short hair was perfectly coifed. Her shoes probably cost a thousand dollars, but even they paled in comparison to the broach she wore at the base of her neck.

"Do you like it?" Her long graceful fingers brushed the diamond-and-ruby pendant that Kat had last seen in Hazel's portrait. "It was my mother-in-law's. It has been given to all the wives of the W. W. Hales for generations." Her gaze slid toward Hale. "Someday it will belong to the wife of my son."

"That's nice," Kat muttered, desperate for something to say.

"I'm so glad you could come today," the woman said.

"You are?" Kat blurted a little too quickly.

"Of course." And then the strangest thing happened. She put her arm around Kat's waist, steered her carefully to a quiet corner of the room. "We were so afraid when Scooter took a leave of absence from school that it would be hard on him. But, honestly, this is bringing us so much closer to our son. And the people in his life."

She gave Kat's waist a tiny squeeze.

"You'll have to come up to the country house, dear. We don't want Scooter losing touch with his friends. Or . . . anyone who might be more than just a friend." She gave a smile, and Kat wondered what kind of alternate reality she had fallen into.

Marcus passed by, and Kat mouthed "help," but he just offered Hale's mother some champagne and continued through the room, wordless.

"And how do you enjoy Knightsbury, Katarina . . . or is it Kat? Which do you prefer?"

For all that she had done in her short life, Kat was not used to playing inside. She didn't know how to smile and flirt, cajole and confuse someone into believing something was their idea (especially when it wasn't). No, Kat was a thief, not a con artist, more her mother's child than her father's in at least that one respect. So it was with a pounding heart and sweaty palms that she told the woman, "Most people call me Kat."

"It is a lovely name." When Hale's mother smiled, Kat felt a pang of familiarity. Hale was built like his father, with the same broad shoulders and tall frame. But right then Kat knew that Hale was actually like his mother. They had the same easy smile and bright eyes. Charm. They were both charmers. And Kat found herself liking the woman just as, years before, she hadn't been able to help liking the boy. It felt a little like she was cheating on Hale. With his mother.

"Isn't that something?"

Kat glanced at Genesis and nodded. "Yes. It really is."

"It's going to be quite impressive when we unveil it at the gala next week. You are coming to the gala, aren't you?"

"Oh, I . . ." Kat looked at Hale, but his mother talked on.

"You simply must. It's such an important night for Scooter. He and his grandmother were very close. Did you know that?"

"Yes," Kat said. She didn't admit that she'd learned it a little too late.

Hale's mother smiled. "The company means a lot to my son, and if I'm correct, *you* mean a lot to my son. I'm the first to admit that he and his father and I have been slightly . . . estranged. He was a challenging boy. But now he's a man, and I want to know him. And I believe it's also important to know you."

"It is?" Kat asked.

Mrs. Hale laughed. "There will be lots of girls who are interested in him now. There were many before, I'm sure, but

136

now . . . well, let's just say this kind of inheritance changes things."

"Not for me," Kat said, and she meant it.

"And that's why I hope that we will be very close, Kat." Hale's mother smiled.

Kat's head was buzzing. No. That wasn't it. The buzzing was reverberating from the center of the crowd.

"The device shouldn't be making that noise," Silas said from across the room.

Kat was more than a little surprised at the speed and agility the old man showed as he raced toward the prototype. There was a loud pop just as he reached it, a burning, hissing spark that sputtered and flamed in a bright arc. Smoke filled the air.

"Foster, what is the meaning of this?" Hale's father snapped as if Silas were deliberately wasting his time.

"I'm not sure," Silas said. "I've personally tested this a dozen times in the past two weeks, and . . . I'm not sure."

Kat looked around the lab at what, if Mr. Foster was correct, was one of the biggest days in the history of Hale Industries. Of the Hale family.

But she couldn't see her Hale anywhere.

Marcus was coming toward her, a tray of shrimp puffs in his hand. But the look in his eyes was enough to stop Kat cold.

"Where is he, Marcus?"

"He's gone to his office."

"Where is it? Please tell me. I have to talk to him."

"No, miss." Marcus took her hand and squeezed. "You have to stop him."

137

CHAPTER 21

Kat wasn't sure what was going on then, but she'd spent too much of her life as the girl with the plan to sit on the sidelines of whatever was happening. She pushed through the halls of Hale Industries, the cubicles and conference rooms spiraling out like a maze, and she didn't know where to go. So she stopped, heart pounding. And listened.

"Gloria, red looks good on you," someone said.

And there he was. Hale was strolling easily down the center aisle, slapping a man on the back and asking, "Hey, Jones, how's the baby?"

"Hale," Kat said, struggling to catch up. "I need to talk to you."

"Go home, Kat," he told her, never breaking stride until he finally came to rest in front of the woman who sat stoically guarding the corner office.

"Mr. Hale," the woman said, a little too much emphasis on the word *Mister* for Kat's liking. "I was not expecting you today."

"Hello, gorgeous." Hale smiled and sat on the corner of the woman's immaculate desk. "I tried to stay away—I really did. But I knew *you* were up here, and I just had to come say hi."

"Delightful," the woman said. "And you brought a guest."

She slid her icy glare from Hale to the girl behind him. Kat shifted and was acutely aware of the fact that the skirt Gabrielle had chosen for her was too short. She wanted to rappel down the elevator shaft and disappear.

"I had to show off the empire. So, have you missed me?" Hale reached down to polish the Hale Industries Employee of the Year plaque that sat beside the woman's computer. "I'm sure you must have missed me."

"It was a struggle, sir. But we've managed."

"Glad to hear it." Hale winked, then he walked toward the wide, sweeping stairs that led to the floor above.

"Go back to the launch, Kat," Hale said once they reached the thirty-eighth floor. This time there was no receptionist, no guard. So Kat and Hale walked, unbothered, to the big mahogany double doors that read W. W. HALE V in gold embossed letters, and Kat recalled what Marcus had told her.

"So, this is your office?" Kat pointed to the words; but then Hale turned the doorknob, pushed, and bumped right into the heavy wood.

"Or not," Kat said when, again, the door didn't budge.

"Seriously, Kat. You can go. Now."

"Not until you talk to me."

Hale pulled a small leather-bound tool kit from the

backpack he carried, and two seconds later, the door was swinging open.

"I'm through talking." He pushed inside a room with plush couches and tall windows, silk curtains, and an oil painting of an English manor. It didn't look like the heart of a cold, corporate world. It was more like a sitting room. A parlor.

Hale walked to the empty desk, plopped the backpack down on top of it, and rummaged inside.

"I like your office," Kat tried again. She couldn't bring herself to face him, so she reached out to let the curtains run through her fingers. "Did you use a decorator?"

"Yeah. My grandmother," Hale said, and Kat went still.

She hadn't thought about exactly where they were, but the reminders were everywhere. The tall bookshelves behind the desk were covered with family photos and books, plaques from assorted charities, and mementos of a life well lived. But only one frame sat on the desk. Kat reached for it, looked down on a fourteen-year-old Hale in a uniform she recognized, a burgundy cardigan over heavy gray trousers.

"I don't miss those sweaters," she said, remembering the way the wool itched against her skin during the three months that she had run from her world to Hale's.

Hale took the photo from her, placed it facedown on the desk. "I don't miss anything from Colgan. Now, if you don't mind, I have a small window and a lot to do."

"What, Hale? What are you going to . . ." But Kat trailed off when she saw what had been in the backpack. Cable and harnesses, a small device used to open windows. Kat's heart began to race.

"Hale, when you said you had work to do, did you mean *your* kind of work or *our* kind of work?"

"What's the matter, Kat?" Hale ran the cable through its harness and secured the other end to a load-bearing beam in the corner of the room. "Don't you like being out of the loop? I know I did."

"Hale, don't—"

"Look at this place, Kat. Look at it!" He reached for a file drawer, threw it open. "Empty," he snapped and moved on to the next one, which was just as hollow. "Nothing. I'm the CEO without any files, the grandson without a clue, and the boyfriend without the whole story."

He moved around the desk until there was nothing between the two of them but secrets and disappointment, and Kat was tired of their weight.

"No one tells me anything. Remember? I'm the guy *everyone* keeps out of the loop."

"That's not fair, Hale," Kat said. "I tried to talk to you about the will."

"When? When did you try?" Hale shouted in frustration. "For crying out loud, Kat. This is my *family*."

"Exactly!" Kat said. "It is your family. And that changes everything. You lose perspective and . . . you can't think straight. When it's personal, Hale, it's dangerous. Trust me."

Kat didn't know what he was doing, she just knew she had to stop him. Or help him. She couldn't let him go alone, even when he opened the office window and climbed onto the ledge. Sloping steel descended beneath him like an icy cliff.

Then Hale hooked the harness around his waist and said, "Look, Kat, you can leave. Or you can help. It makes no difference to me."

And then he spread out his arms. And jumped.

CHAPTER 22

"Whose office is this?" Kat asked the moment she was inside.

"Guess," Hale said, but she didn't really have to. There was a photo of Garrett and Natalie on the corner of the desk, but even without it, Kat would have known.

"Hale, I don't think this is a good idea."

"Really? Because I think it's my only idea," he snapped, then softened. "You're right, okay? I'll say it. Something is wrong. Now, let's find out what."

"Then why don't we come back later—get Simon and Gabrielle and . . . Hale, let's just think about this."

"I'm through thinking, Kat. Garrett is at the launch *for now*. So the way I see it, we've got fifteen—maybe twenty minutes to do this. You can help, or—"

"What do you want me to do?"

The to-do list was simple enough. They'd spent enough time with Simon to know how to bypass the man's password and access his computer. They could plant their video cameras in the heating vents, and after a few minutes with the phone system, they would be able to overhear every call he made or received on the company line. The fax number could be cloned and the Internet piggybacked. It all should have been easy enough, but Kat could feel Hale's presence, hear his breath. He was still the boy who had stormed off in London, and even in that tiny office, it was like there was an ocean between them.

Hale neither moved nor spoke for a long time, until finally he asked, "What does he want?"

Kat took a fresh look at the room around her. It was far smaller than she would have expected. The desk. The shelves. Even the view seemed less impressive than the one just a story above.

"He's not decorating like a man who wants to be top dog," Kat said.

"No." Hale reached for the painting behind the desk, slid it aside to reveal the wall-mounted safe hidden behind it. "He's decorating like a man with things to hide."

Three minutes later, Kat was still working on the lock.

"Come on, Kat," Hale said. "Can you get it, or—"

"Got it," Kat said, standing back and letting the safe door swing open. She reached into the safe and pulled out a stack of accordion-style folders.

"Bingo." She tossed the folders onto the desk. "Oh, Garrett, you have been a bad, bad boy."

"Not him," Hale said, staring into a folder. "Us."

143

Kat couldn't help herself. She reached gingerly for another one, saw the name *Elizabeth* written on it in big black letters.

"What is it?" she asked.

"There's a folder here for every member of Hazel's family," Hale said. He reached into one, pulled out a black-and-white photograph, and tilted his head. "That's my uncle Joe," Hale said. "And that is *not* my aunt Olivia."

Kat picked up the folder labeled *Senior.* "What are these, bank records?" She did a double take, looking at Hale. "Did your dad really pay two million dollars to the campaign to elect Ross Perot?"

"I . . ." Hale said, stumbling for words and thumbing through another file. "Wow. Well, I guess my cousin Charlotte isn't actually my cousin."

"Don't worry," Kat said. "It looks like there might be a kid in Queens who is."

"Do I want to know why Garrett has a news clipping from a hit-and-run on New Year's Eve 2001?" Hale asked a moment later.

"I don't get it," Kat said. "How does he know all this? Some of these go back decades."

"His dad," Hale said softly. "Cleaning up Hale family messes has been the Garrett family business for fifty years. He knows everything."

When Kat finally reached the bottom of the stack, she stood for a long time, staring at the final folder, the one labeled *Scooter.*

"Well, let's see what skeletons I have in my closet," Hale said, and Kat prepared herself for anything. Nothing at all would have surprised her except for the sight of Hale holding the file upside down. "Empty."

It shouldn't have scared her, but it did. Not that Hale had a file, but that Garrett had seen fit to empty it at some point in time. And as Kat replaced the files in the safe and tidied up the desk, she couldn't help but wonder what other secrets might lie out there, waiting like a trap that was set to spring.

"You know what this means, Hale," Kat warned as she took one last look around the office to make sure their tracks were clean. "You know we have to be careful."

"I don't want to be careful."

"There!" Kat snapped. "That's why I didn't tell you what was going on. That's—"

But a voice came seeping through the door, cutting Kat off, saying, "Hello, Mr. Garrett."

The small light on the panel next to the door flashed green. The door began to open. And Kat knew that they had been caught.

"Oh, Mr. Garrett," said another voice from outside, and the door stopped. "We need to talk about the launch."

Kat glanced around the room. Paneling hid a pocket door and, behind that, a tiny closet.

"In here," she said, pulling open the closet door and pushing Hale inside. They stood squeezed together, but there wasn't room to shift, much less slip away.

"What can I do for you, Foster?" Garrett asked.

It's Silas, Kat realized, but she couldn't move or think or breathe. The office door opened, and there was the sound of footsteps entering.

"The gala is next week. . . ."

"I know," Garrett said.

"I came to ask you . . . to beg you . . . to put it off."

Garrett laughed. "Why would we do that?"

There was a long pause. Kat could imagine the look on Silas's face as he said, "Well, Mr. Garrett, we're supposed to unveil Genesis to the public that night. And the prototype didn't work."

"No, Silas," Garrett said. "It didn't. But if we delay, Hale Industries' stock will drop another twenty points."

"Show up with a faulty prototype and twenty points will be a drop in the bucket. If we just push the gala back a few months or—"

"*Months?* Are you insane? This launch has been in the works since before Mrs. Hale passed, and in Mrs. Hale's honor, we will—"

"Don't do this." Silas's voice was hard. "Don't pretend you're doing this for Hazel. Give me time to fix the prototype. Give me time to make this right."

"You've had time. You've had years. And now we have to go on as planned."

"Listen to me!" There was a loud slap, as if Silas had banged his hand against the desk. "Something is wrong. I'm begging you. Give us time to fix it."

"The prototype *looks* fine, Silas," Garrett said. "It will be fine."

"Hazel never would have done this." There was a new edge to Silas's voice. "She never would have compromised the future of this company out of pride."

"Yes. But, unfortunately, Hazel is dead." Kat could have sworn she felt Hale's heart beat faster. "Now, you do have a point," Garrett went on. "The prototype doesn't work, and that does have to change things."

"Of course it does," Silas said.

"So I think I should probably let the man responsible go."

"Excuse me?"

"Clean out your desk, Silas. It's time for you to retire."

"The board—"

"The board acts in an advisory capacity. And given what they've just seen, I'm certain they would advise me to show you the door. So there it is."

"If you want to fire me, Mr. Garrett, I suppose I can't stop you, but this is a mistake."

"You're right about one thing. You can't stop me."

A door slammed, and a moment later, Kat heard Garrett say, "Louise?"

"Yes, Mr. Garrett?" The assistant's voice boomed through the office on speakerphone.

"Please let Human Resources know that Mr. Foster is no longer with Hale Industries. And call security. Tell them to be on the lookout. We don't need any uninvited guests walking around."

Kat tensed.

"Very well," the woman said. "I have some forms that need your signature. Shall I bring them in?"

"No. I'll come out there."

The door opened and closed, and for a few seconds they were alone. Hale's breath was warm on Kat's skin. She could feel the rise and fall of his chest, and she wanted to kiss him, hold him, breathe him in. She wanted to go back to Argentina. For a split second, he looked down at her, and she knew he was feeling that way too. Anger and grief pounded together. There were too many emotions for such a small space, and the result was electric.

"Kat . . ." he sighed her name.

"I'm sorry, Hale. I'm sorry I didn't tell you. And I'm sorry . . . I'm just sorry, okay?"

He didn't say it was okay. He didn't tell her she was forgiven. He just sank to the cold, hard floor and pulled his knees to his chest, like a little boy hiding in his father's closet.

They couldn't leave without being heard, couldn't turn on a light without being seen, so Kat joined him on the floor and whispered, "What do we do now?"

"We wait."

Over the next several hours, they heard Garrett typing on his keyboard. He made a series of overseas calls and spoke badly accented Chinese and French, a little German that Kat was able to pick up. But mostly she just sat, waiting.

Eventually she felt herself leaning against Hale, and he didn't protest. The night grew longer, and Kat's head grew heavier, and at some point she must have rested on his chest. She closed her eyes. Hale's arms were warm and comforting around her, and there was no place else she wanted to be.

"Kat." Hale's whisper broke into her thoughts, but she didn't stir. "Kat." He shook her shoulder. "I think he's gone."

Part of Kat knew she should have felt foolish for falling asleep on the job, but another part was so happy to have Hale's arms around her, to feel his breath on her skin.

"Hi," she told him.

"Hi, yourself," he said.

Still half asleep and groggy, Kat squinted up through the shadows of the tiny space and into Hale's eyes. It was the closest they'd been in weeks. Whatever had stood between them was lost in the shadows, and Kat felt Hale's mouth press against hers. His fingers wove into her hair, holding her close, gripping her tightly. It was the hungriest kiss she'd ever known, and Kat let herself get lost in it. Forget. Tell herself that there was nothing they couldn't do as long as they were together.

But, then again, they were currently trapped in a closet on the thirty-seventh floor of a well-secured high-rise in the middle of the night, so perhaps her judgment was lacking.

"Sorry," Hale said, breaking the kiss and pulling away.

"No, Hale," Kat said one more time, "I'm sorry. I should have told you about the will as soon as I heard."

"Let's just get out of here, okay?" He struggled to his feet and pressed an ear against the door. A moment later he was pushing out into the dark cold office and gesturing for Kat to follow.

The door was monitored by security, so they found a ceiling vent and made their escape that way, crawling until they reached another grate. Hale jumped down onto a desk below, and when Kat dropped, he caught her, held her there.

"You okay?" he asked.

She nodded.

"So what happens now?"

It was an excellent question, and Kat wasn't quite sure how to answer.

"I think we're going to need someone who knows more about the company than we do. Someone inside. Maybe your parents? Your mom seemed nice."

"My mom's a better con artist than I am."

"What about Silas? We could tell him."

A small light flickered on. "Tell me what?"

CHAPTER 23

As a general rule, getting caught is never, ever good. It was the first rule of the family, so Kat didn't know whether to feel ashamed or embarrassed, angry or relieved, as they stood on a gleaming stainless steel table in the big room.

"Silas, have you been here all night?" Kat asked.

His suit coat hung over the back of a chair, and his bow tie was loose around his neck. Papers and drawings were scattered on the desk in front of him, and Kat could see a half-empty takeout container and tall cup of coffee.

"Funny," Silas said. "I could be asking the same of you." In spite of the hour and the circumstances, he gave a nervous giggle. "If you don't mind my saying, Mr. Hale. She's a keeper." He pointed in Kat's direction.

It was undeniable, Kat thought. Silas was a dork. And Kat couldn't help herself—she liked him. A lot.

In the pale light of a desk lamp, Kat watched Silas's eyes as he looked around the room. There were polished tables and carefully organized workstations. Whiteboards covered one entire wall, each filled with mathematical formulas and chemical equations. It was a language Kat couldn't begin to understand. But like any good con artist, Kat was fluent in the language of people.

"Silas," she said, "what's going on?"

"I love this lab. I am going to miss it now that I am no longer in your employ, Mr. Hale. Thought I'd pull one last all-nighter in here." Silas studied Hale. "Why do I get the feeling you aren't surprised to hear that?"

"Garrett can't do this," Hale was saying. "He can't just . . . fire you. You—"

"Created Genesis?" Silas filled in. "The product that didn't work? The biggest embarrassment in the history of this company? Yes. I'm that guy. And I'm currently unemployed." He gave an odd little bow, then added with a wink, "Of course, I'm also the guy who designed the security system, so they can't keep me out. Yet."

"So Genesis had a glitch," Hale said. "It will work eventually."

"No, Mr. Hale. *It did work.* It worked perfectly. In fact, the last time I spoke to your grandmother, it was to tell her that I was finished. I tested it myself. And then I put it in there." He spun and pointed to a safe.

"Silas," Hale said, "are you saying . . ."

"Whatever it was we saw at the launch, it wasn't the prototype I made. No, sir. I just don't know how anyone could have switched them. I kept the prototype locked up until the moment of the demonstration." He walked over to the safe. "I

151

just can't figure out how they got inside this. It's state of the art," the man added.

"Do you mind?" Kat asked, and Silas stepped aside.

"What do you think?" Hale asked.

Kat ran a finger along the inner workings of the lock. "It's been tampered with," she said. "By someone pretty good."

"And you know this because . . ." Silas prompted.

"I have hobbies," Kat told him. "Seriously, Silas, someone who knew what they were doing was in here."

"Well, at least I was robbed by a professional." Silas dropped onto a stool almost as if his body couldn't support the weight of his disappointment.

"Can't you make another prototype?" Hale asked.

"Eventually. Maybe. But it wouldn't do you or the company any good, Mr. Hale. That's why I came to plead with Garrett. If the faulty prototype is unveiled at the gala, then I'm afraid of what will happen. To the company." He leveled Hale with a look. "To all of us."

"I'll get you whatever you need, Silas. Just make me another prototype."

"It's not going to be that simple. After tonight I'll no longer have a lab."

"I'll get you a lab."

"And the plans are supposed to be stored on the company server, but they've been tampered with. My personal backup drives have been erased. Someone wants Genesis to disappear, Mr. Hale. And me with it."

"What if we can recover the plans?" Kat asked. Silas raised his eyebrows, doubtful. So Kat shrugged and added, "We know a computer guy."

"Oh, you do, do you?"

"Yes," Kat said. She got the feeling that Silas was a man who saw right through her and actually liked what he was seeing.

"Your computer guy is welcome to try," Silas said. "But it's gone. Everything is gone."

Hale said nothing. Kat saw that he was studying the whiteboards. She wondered for a moment if he was reading the math and the formulas, trying to fix a problem she didn't even understand. But then he pointed to a list in the corner of one of the boards.

"That's my grandmother's handwriting," Hale said, staring at the words.

Silas nodded. "It is."

"She wanted this to work, didn't she?"

"Very much," Silas said.

"Okay," Hale said. "He can fire you, but I can rehire you. Don't worry, Silas. First thing tomorrow I'll—"

"You'll what?" Silas cut Hale off. "With all due respect, Scooter, Garrett is still the trustee and you're still a minor. You're a bright boy. Your grandmother loved you, so I love you, but until you come of age, I'm afraid there's nothing you *can* do."

Silas thought it was over. Kat could see it in his eyes. His shoulders were slumped and his hands trembled. And Kat thought he was probably going to stay at that desk until morning and the guards came to carry him away. He was making his last stand in the only way he knew how.

Fortunately, Kat and Hale knew another way.

"We can get your prototype back," Kat said, coming to stand next to Hale.

"And how are you going to do that?" the old man asked. Hale smiled. "That's easy, Silas. We can steal it."

The sun was not yet up over New York City when the owner of Hale Industries emerged from the building's side entrance, a shorter-than-average teenage girl at his side.

A chill had settled into the air overnight, and as they walked, he removed his jacket and placed it around her thin shoulders. And there, in the middle of the city, the two of them were almost alone. Two kids who were out far too late or far too early, walking down a cracked and vacant sidewalk like they owned it.

"It was Marcus, wasn't it?" Hale asked. "Who hired you?"

"Don't be mad at him. He was just—"

Hale cut her off with a shake of his head. "He was right. You were right. These aren't Hazel's wishes."

He stopped and looked up at the towering building that bore his name. The faintest hint of sunlight was creeping over the horizon, and with it, the whole building seemed to glow.

"We almost got caught, didn't we?"

"Yeah." Kat laughed a little. "But we didn't."

"You had a good point in there. Breaking in like that was stupid. I was stupid."

"Hale, stop it." Kat reached out and grabbed his arm. "You are many things, but stupid isn't one of them."

"I'm too close."

"You don't get it, do you? Being close is good. Caring is good. I love that you're emotional and passionate and can't turn these things off."

"It makes me a bad thief."

"It makes you a good person."

Of all the things Hale had been told in his life, Kat wondered if anyone had ever told him that.

He gave her his trademark grin. "So, what do you say, Miss Bishop? Want to steal a prototype?"

"Re-steal," Kat corrected. "These days I only re-steal. Besides, I'm not entirely sure you can afford me."

"Oh, I bet we can work something out."

"And there is the matter of—"

But then Kat couldn't finish because Hale's lips had found hers. When they parted, he grew serious.

"You will steal it, won't you?"

"*We* will." She looked down the street. "Just as soon as we find it."

5 DAYS BEFORE THE GALA

NEW YORK, NEW YORK, USA

CHAPTER 24

In a city of eight million people, it is easy enough to go unseen. Anonymity is perhaps the island of Manhattan's greatest asset, and it came even easier for Garrett than for most.

The residents of the high-rise apartment building on the Upper East Side knew only that he rose early and lived alone. He received no packages and, aside from a daughter, had no guests, and on the rare occasion that one of his neighbors might share the elevator with him either early in the morning or late at night, he would simply nod and study the newspaper that seemed perpetually tucked under one arm.

He neither made nor complained of noise, did not decorate for any holidays, and the children of his building didn't even bother knocking at Halloween.

What Garrett did, it seemed, was work, and in New York

City, this made him not the least bit special.

The people at his coffee shop expected him at seven-fifteen; he bought his morning bagel promptly at half past.

To all of these people (and then some), he was simply known as The Man in the Hat as he walked to and from the Hale Industries office in a gray felt fedora, rain or shine, in every month except July (during which time he wore no hat at all).

The people at the coffee shop thought The Man in the Hat was some kind of throwback, an extra from a TV show, perhaps. But on this particular Friday morning, there was at least one person on the streets who knew better.

Kat was quietly sitting in the shadows of a café window when Garrett's doorman greeted him, but she didn't bother to cross and follow. Gabrielle was in place at the corner, and besides, they already knew the route. What they needed to know was the man.

When he cut through the park, Gabrielle was a safe distance behind, and Kat was left alone to pull his trash from the dumpster and pick the lock on his mailbox. And when, twelve hours later, the man was still not home, even Kat had to admit that the day had basically come to nothing.

He cleaned his own apartment, collected his own dry cleaning, and his bills and financial records were done exclusively online. He neither drank nor smoked, didn't date or socialize. According to the building's official records, the Garrett apartment had no safe and no storage lockers. What it did have was a state-of-the-art security system and a nosy neighbor who kept her hearing aids turned up as high as they would go.

The one thing Kat knew was that she had to get into that apartment. Exactly how, however, was an entirely different story.

So that's why Kat was standing in the shadows of the building across the street, thinking, scheming, when a voice caught her completely off guard.

"Kat?"

She pivoted on the sidewalk, knowing exactly who she was going to find.

"Hey," Natalie said with a smile. "I thought that was you."

"Natalie, hi," Kat told her. "What are you doing here?"

"I live there." Natalie pointed to the building Kat had been staring at for most of the day.

"Wow," Kat said. "Small world. I was just on my way . . ." But Kat didn't bother to finish, because Nat was already crossing the street.

"You wanna come up?" she asked.

"Yeah," Kat said. "I'd love to."

It wasn't the first time Kat had been invited inside a place she was trying to rob. Part of her knew she should have felt guilty about the invitation, but she couldn't quite summon the emotion.

Standing in the elevator next to Natalie, it wasn't hard to see her as Hale saw her. She had an easy smile and a nice laugh, and Kat could imagine her as a little girl, running with a little Hale through Hazel's big old house. Two children bringing life to that half-dead building. That is, before Kat came and took Hale away.

"So . . ." Natalie seemed almost afraid of the question. "How is he?"

The elevator doors slid open and Kat followed the girl toward apartment D, acting like she'd never been in the building before.

"I'm not sure." Kat shrugged. "He still seems . . . sad."

"Yeah." Natalie put her key in the door but didn't turn it. "Hazel was awesome. Scoot is awesome. And they seemed to be the only people in the whole family who knew that about each other. You know?"

But Kat didn't know. Hale's family was an enigma. She'd never met Hazel. And "Scooter" was a stranger Kat couldn't even start to reconcile with the boy she knew. She thought about the night before, about Hale's arms around her, the way his fingers played with her hair. And she prayed she never had to. She hoped that maybe Scooter might be gone for good.

"Oh well," Natalie said. She pushed open the door and rushed to punch out a nine-digit code on the keypad.

"Wow," Kat said. "That's a lot of numbers for a security code."

"Tell me about it. My dad is totally paranoid. He's probably got cameras watching us right now," Natalie teased, and Kat took a surreptitious turn around the room. She didn't see any of the usual models, but in a private residence, with so many hiding places, a person could never be sure.

"So, this is a nice place," she told the girl.

"It's not mine," Nat said. "It's my dad's, and he's . . . well . . . we're looking for some new school to take me." She stretched out on the sofa. "Do you want a drink or something?"

"No thank you."

"You're so polite, Cute Kat. It's sweet. Your mother must be very proud."

"She's dead," Kat blurted the words. It was so weird to talk about her mother with a stranger that she honestly didn't know how. "I mean, she died. When I was little."

"I'm sorry," Natalie said, taken aback. "Mine's in Florida.

Remarried." She had the look of someone who thought her own mother might as well be dead but didn't dare to say so.

So Kat just kept studying the room. There was a utilitarian couch and chair. There were prints on the wall by American artists, a TV ten years out of date, which Kat guessed was never used.

"I know why you're here."

The words came quickly, like a slap. And Kat reeled with them for a moment until Natalie went on. "I don't think you were just passing by, were you? I think you were hoping to run into me."

Kat blushed. "I guess maybe I was."

"I think you wanted to ask me about Scooter." Nat placed her legs on the coffee table and crossed them. When she smiled, she had a particularly devious look in her eye. "After all, I know where all the bodies are buried."

Natalie laughed a little, but Kat just thought about the folders in Natalie's father's office. She wondered what the folder labeled *Scooter* might have had to say.

"So there are bodies, are there?" Kat asked.

Natalie nodded. "Lots of them. Poor guy couldn't keep a pet if his life depended on it. That rose garden has got to have at least a half dozen gerbils."

Kat smiled at the thought. She herself had never had a pet, unless you counted the time the Bagshaws' father had needed her to dog-sit Queen Elizabeth's favorite corgi.

"You want popcorn?" Natalie asked, standing up. "I want popcorn."

"Sure," Kat said, moving on to a bookshelf full of classics, eyeing every one in turn; but nothing about the books was fake. The prototype was small. Portable. Great for hiding, hard for finding. At least now that Kat had the security code she could always come back later.

"Butter?" Natalie called.

"Absolutely!" Kat said.

"Make yourself at home," Natalie said, and Kat did as she was told, helping herself to the bathroom, joining Nat in the kitchen, then walking back to the living room, positioning it all within the framework of everything she knew.

Garrett was a meticulous man, and as a result, he kept a meticulous house. In the bathroom, the towels were perfectly straight. What little food there was in the kitchen was carefully labeled. The whole apartment smelled of Windex and Lemon Pledge, and Kat could imagine that he'd spent so much of life cleaning up other people's messes that he didn't know when or how to stop.

The only thing slightly out of order was a stack of papers on the coffee table. Kat could imagine him dropping them there after work one night. Some junk mail and a takeout menu, phone bill, bank statement . . .

Passport.

"Natalie," Kat said, reaching for it, "are you going back to Europe already?"

"What? Oh that." Natalie glanced at the passport and pushed the thought aside. "No. That's my dad's. Has some business trip tomorrow."

"That's cool. Where?"

"Hong Kong," Natalie said, then crinkled her nose. "I think."

And Kat couldn't help herself: she peeked at the piece of paper tucked inside the small blue booklet, at the word *Aviary* circled in red. And the time: eight o'clock.

4 DAYS UNTIL
THE GALA

HONG KONG,
CHINA

CHAPTER 25

Kat had never felt at home in Hong Kong. Sure, she and her father had lived there for eight months after her mother died. The two of them had spent hours walking through the massive tide of people that ebbed and flowed, beating like a pulse through the city's center. But no matter what, her mother's memory followed them everywhere. Despite their best efforts, they were never quite able to lose her.

That was the thought that kept pounding in her head that afternoon. Gabrielle was at her back, Hale fifty feet behind her, and the three of them stayed on the crowded sidewalk, following the man in the hat. She kept her eyes forward and her pace steady. Gabrielle split off and took the other side of the street while Kat stepped out of the way of a bicycle. She got jostled by a food vendor moving a cart full of very strange-looking oranges. But she kept the man in her sights until, finally, he turned off the busy street and into Hong Kong Park.

"Kat?" Hale's voice was in her ear. "Where is he? Did you—"

"She didn't lose him," Gabrielle said.

"Where is he going?" Hale asked.

"We don't know." Gabrielle sounded annoyed. "That's why we're *following* him."

"But—"

"Hale, does someone need to go back to the hotel?" Gabrielle scolded him as if he were a little boy.

But Hale didn't answer, and Kat walked deeper into the park. Concrete gave way to mossy grass. She moved from the shadow of buildings to the shadow of trees, and a cool breeze blew across her skin, carrying with it a sound that was growing louder and louder with every step.

"What's that noise?" Gabrielle asked.

"I don't know, Gabs. I think . . ." But Kat trailed off as soon as she saw the massive net suspended within the trees and finally knew exactly what she was seeing.

"Birds." Kat thought of the note in the man's apartment. "Garrett is going to see the birds."

That was as far as Hale could go, Gabrielle said, and Kat couldn't argue with the logic. There was a reason clients never went on jobs, so Gabrielle waited outside with Hale, and Kat followed Garrett into the aviary alone.

As Kat walked down the winding paths, the sound was overwhelming. Birds chirped and sang, filling the air. Kat couldn't hear anything over their cries. Not the crunch of the gravel beneath her feet or even the sound of Hale arguing with Gabrielle in her ear.

She was utterly alone in that huge faux forest until the trees parted, and she saw Garrett. He gripped the wooden railing of a footbridge, staring up at the skyline that peeked through the canopy of trees.

"Okay, guys," Kat said into her comms, "I found him. Looks like he's waiting for something or . . ." She paused as another man stepped onto the bridge. "Someone."

The man greeted Garrett with a bow. He wore a dark suit and dark glasses, but their words were lost to Kat beneath the cries of the birds around them.

A smaller path branched away from the main walkway, twisting through the trees and passing beneath the footbridge overhead, so Kat crept toward it. The birds squawked above. A brightly colored pair flew away when she approached their perch, but the men didn't seem to notice, because they talked on, and eventually Kat could make out the words.

"You have the device?" the other man asked.

"I do."

"May I see it, please?"

Garrett huffed. "I don't have it on me, of course. But it's someplace I can access very easily when the time comes."

"And it's secure there?" the man asked. "The Hales are powerful people. If they suspect what you've done, they will try to retrieve it, will they not?"

Garrett leaned against the railing and stared out through the net at the skyscrapers that loomed not far away and laughed. It was a cold, dry sound. "Oh, I assure you, the Hales have never bothered with the business before. I see no reason for them to start now. And, besides . . . I have placed the prototype in a place where nothing has been stolen. Ever. So, yes, it is safe."

"And you can get it?"

"Sir, it is right under my nose. So close that it could be yours as soon as you pay my asking price."

"And have the Hales reveal their prototype at the gala next week?" Now it was the buyer's turn to laugh. "I don't think so."

"The Hales won't be a problem," Garrett told him.

"Perhaps. But a wise man is a cautious man. I will wait to see what becomes of the Hales and their prototype. As soon as the world knows they have not mastered the Genesis technology, then—and only then—you and I will have a deal."

Garrett didn't argue. He just said his good-byes, and when he finally left the aviary, Kat didn't bother to follow. She had seen and heard all she needed to know. So she stumbled out of the park alone. She closed her eyes and thought about the view out of Hale's office window, the sprawling streets below. It must have been like working in a cloud. A celestial view.

Then she thought about her trip to Garrett's apartment, the carefully organized shelves and perfectly straight pictures—not a thing out of place except for the pile of mail that lay discarded on the table. It had seemed strange, Kat had thought at the time. Something about the sight had stayed with her—the one little bit of disorder in his otherwise perfect world.

But that wasn't it. She knew it then. So she closed her eyes and thought about the letters and bills and the bank statement addressed to the man who did all of his banking online.

"Hale," Kat said cautiously through the comms, "there's a bank next door to your building, right?"

"Yeah." Hale sounded nervous. "Why?"

"Which one?"

"Superior Bank of Manhattan," he told her, and Kat's heart sank. She'd known that would be the answer. A part of her had feared it from the moment she saw the bank statement lying on Garrett's coffee table, as soon as she'd heard his words on the bridge.

"Earth to Kitty," Gabrielle said. "Are you going to tell us what's wrong?"

"Kat?" Hale yelled.

And Kat took a deep breath. "This is bad. This is very, very bad."

3 DAYS UNTIL THE GALA

SOMEWHERE NORTH OF PARIS

CHAPTER 26

The train car wasn't quite large enough, but no one seemed to mind. It was secluded and safe, and there was something about the lull of a locomotive, the gentle rock and sway and the blur of countryside, that had always been conducive to thinking, in Katarina Bishop's humble opinion. So she sat with her legs curled up beneath her and let Hale take the lead, standing at the front of the car.

"Thanks for coming, everyone," he told them.

"Of course we came," Simon said.

"I want you all to know that this is not an ordinary job, and I know that. I'll pay you for your time and—"

"You think I'm here for money?" Gabrielle said.

"Now, now, Gabs. Let the man speak." Angus slipped an arm around her shoulders. Gabrielle elbowed him in the gut.

He winced and corrected, "I mean, anything for a friend."

Angus gave a smile, and Hale talked on.

"I know this isn't a typical heist, but I've got to try something, and the people I trust most are in this car. So we can do it. I know we can."

"Forgive me, Hale my boy"—Hamish inched a tiny bit closer—"but what exactly is *it*?"

This time Hale looked at Kat and shrugged, the universal signal for *Do you want to take this one or should I?* So Kat turned to the group. "As you know, Marcus came to me after Hazel died and told us that something was off with the will."

Kat glanced at Marcus, who stood silently in the corner, like always. But it wasn't like always. Not by a long shot. "Mrs. Hale had made a promise to my sister," the butler said. "And Mrs. Hale was a woman who always kept her promises."

The group gave a nod, and Marcus silently returned to attention. He'd said all he had to say.

"Yeah," Kat said, taking up the story. "So the working theory is that Garrett changed the will so that Hale would inherit the company." She spoke as plainly as she could. She wanted to be cool. Emotionless. She had to spit it out, get over the fact that one of her own had been the mark.

"As long as Hale is a minor, then Garrett can be the trustee and call the shots. It's a long con," she told them. Then she had to admit: "And a good one."

An air of respect seemed to fill the car. They didn't like Garrett. But that didn't mean they couldn't see the genius in such a simple plan.

"So," Angus asked, "what do you need us to do?"

Kat nodded at Gabrielle, who placed a pile of papers and photographs on the table in the center of the car.

"This is Genesis," Kat said. Immediately, Simon grabbed the pictures, and Kat talked on. "It's the newest product out of Hale Industries. The prototype and all of the design schematics are missing. We think Garrett switched them out for fakes, which leaves him free to sell the *real* Genesis to this man." A photo Gabrielle had taken in Hong Kong landed on the top of the pile.

"Who is he?" Simon asked.

"He is the head of Research and Development for one of the biggest tech companies in Asia," Hale said. "And one of Hale Industries' biggest competitors. Our sources tell us they've been trying to develop something like Genesis for years, but they can't get theirs to work— What?" He cut a grin at Kat when he saw the impressed look on her face. "Corporate espionage is my second great passion."

"With your first being . . ." Kat prompted.

"Gelato," Hale said, and turned back to the group. "So Garrett stole the prototype and the designs. He plans to sell them, pocket the profits, and sink my company. We think." He shrugged a little, as if the man's exact motives didn't matter. And they didn't. None of it would change what they had to do, so Hale smiled and raised an eyebrow. "That's why we're going to steal them back."

"Wait. Far be it for me to say this"—Hamish looked around the compartment—"and if anyone tells Uncle Eddie I suggested being an upstanding citizen I'll kill 'em, but aren't there . . . laws and stuff? I mean, can't you . . . you know . . . sue him or something?" asked the boy who had once stolen an entire circus, all three rings.

"You'd think so," Kat explained. "But according to what we got off of Garrett's computer, the patent office has a bogus design on file for the Genesis plans. That means that if and when the *real* Genesis turns up from some other company, Hale Industries won't have a legal leg to stand on. Needless to say, it's handy when the person responsible for protecting the design is the same person intent on stealing it."

"We're in the wrong business," Angus said.

Simon nodded. "So true."

"The bad news is time. We've got to get the prototype and design back *now*," Kat said.

"Why?" Angus asked.

"Because Hale Industries is dangerously low on working capital," Gabrielle said. "The return on investment of the last five products has been less than one percent, and without a major influx of cash from subcontracts and the buzz that a hot new product can bring, the share price is going to go through the basement."

Everyone stared at her.

"What?" Gabrielle raised an eyebrow. "I've conned *a lot* of MBAs. So Garrett plans to sell the Genesis prototype and its blueprints to the competition, make a fortune, and destroy Hale's family all in one blow?"

"Two birds," Hamish started.

"One stone," Angus finished.

"If I didn't hate this guy so much, I might kind of idolize him," Hamish said. "Is that wrong?"

No one answered.

"The good news is that we know what he's doing now— what his endgame is." Suddenly the car was too stuffy. Kat wanted to open a window. "Yesterday, Gab and Hale and I followed Garrett to his meeting with the buyer. Something he said led us to believe that he has stashed the prototype and plans in a safety deposit box." She took a deep breath. "At the Superior Bank of Manhattan."

Angus's face broke into a wide grin. "I'm sorry, Kitty, but I thought you said it was in the Superior Bank of Manhattan."

"I did," Kat told him, but she didn't exactly feel like smiling back.

"The Superior Bank of Manhattan?" Simon said. "*The* Superior Bank of Manhattan? The *Superior Bank* of—"

"Yeah, Simon," Gabrielle said, cutting him off. "That's the one."

"It's going to take resources," Kat said.

Hale nodded. "Done. What else?"

"People. More than are in this car," she said.

"Please." Gabrielle gave a dismissive wave, and crossed her long legs. "What else?"

But the final thing, Kat seemed almost afraid to say.

"Time." She swallowed hard. "There is no way to steal the prototype before the launch—not if it's at the Superior Bank of Manhattan. Their security is too good and . . . it's the Superior Bank of Manhattan. No one has ever done it."

"That's what they said last time. . . ." Hamish said.

"And the time before," Angus added.

"The Cleopatra Emerald was being moved, and that made it vulnerable. We had two weeks for the Henley," Kat countered. "The launch is in three *days*. I don't know . . ."

"So we *steal* time," Hale said. His words had a force to them. And for a second, they scared her. Then Hale softened, retreated. "So what do you say, Kat?"

She nodded, but it took her a moment to mutter, "Okay.

We just have to delay the launch, right? We can do that. We just have to . . ." But she let her voice trail off, absolutely unsure what to say.

"I don't see what the problem is." Gabrielle stretched out on a bench. "We can find Garrett, right? And he can't sell the prototype if he is . . . shall we say . . . tied up?" She gave a self-satisfied smirk.

"Gabrielle!" Kat rolled her eyes.

"What?" Her cousin looked as innocent as she could possibly be. "We could keep him someplace nice. It will be like a vacation. Or rehab. He might even thank us."

"Yeah," Kat mocked. "Thank us . . . have us arrested for kidnapping . . . really, they're practically the same thing."

Gabrielle huffed. "You have obviously never conned anyone in rehab."

On the other side of the car, Hamish slapped his thigh and proclaimed, "I like it!"

"Of course you do," Kat said.

"Now, now, hear me out," Hamish went on. "We don't have to kidnap Garrett. Not if we kidnap the *buyer*."

"Or distract him," Angus added.

"Like the Bulgari job," Hamish said.

"You mean the job that landed half the DiMarco family in a South African prison?" Kat said.

Angus shrugged. "Nobody said it was perfect."

"You're missing the point, guys," Kat told them. "We have to get the prototype back before the launch. If the investors and stockholders see the faulty model . . ."

"Hale Industries is finished," Hale said.

"The Princess and the Pea?" Gabrielle suggested.

"Not enough time," Kat said.

"Where's Waldo?" Gabrielle went on.

"No." Hamish recoiled. "I am still not allowed back in Morocco."

"Three Blind Mice?" Simon said.

Everyone looked at Kat, who shivered. "I don't do rodents."

The train kept going and the suggestions kept flying, but none found their mark, and finally silence descended on the crew.

"Maybe we're making it too hard," Simon said. "Simple is good, right?"

"As long as we're not kidnapping anyone," Kat said.

Gabrielle blushed. "It was only a suggestion."

"What do we know about Garrett?" Kat asked. "Hale, does he gamble?"

"I don't think so," Hale said with a shake of his head.

"Drink?" Kat asked.

"No more than any of the other people from my childhood."

"Chase the ladies?" Hamish asked.

"No. He's just . . . a lawyer. He was always there. Briefcase. Suit. Hat. The guy is seriously boring. There is nothing scandalous or even interesting about him."

"Well, that's not exactly true." Kat spoke softly, carefully. She forced herself to meet Hale's gaze. "He does have an ex-wife. And a daughter."

"Natalie isn't a part of this. She isn't," Hale insisted even when Kat didn't protest.

"Okay. I believe you," Kat said. "But she might be useful."

"We're not going to use her." Hale's voice was like stone, unmoving. "And besides, it's not like she and her dad are exactly close. Natalie went away to boarding school when her

181

parents divorced. She hardly ever came home after that."

"How long has Garrett worked for the company?" Gabrielle asked.

"That's the thing." Hale shrugged. "There's always been *a Garrett* working for us. His dad had the job before him, and so he was always . . . around."

"Okay, so we go farther back." Kat felt herself swaying, rocking like the train. "Tell us about your grandfather."

"What can I say, Kat? He's dead. They're all dead. My grandmother. My grandfather. My grandfather's brother—"

"Wait," Kat said. "Was this the brother who was supposed to run the company with your grandfather?"

"Yeah. He died way before I was born. He was supposed to be a real character, but then he died, and my grandfather got it all—all the money, but all the pressure and responsibility too. He was a workaholic. And—"

"When did your great-uncle die?" Kat asked.

"Maybe fifty years ago. Like I said, I never knew him. No one ever talked about him. It was like the whole family thought he was cursed or something."

"No more curses." Gabrielle's whole body shivered. "Please no more curses."

"It wasn't that kind of curse, Gabs," Hale told her. "He was just . . . I don't know . . . super eccentric or something. He wanted to be famous, but famous in a way that had nothing to do with being a *Hale*. So he was always doing stuff like climbing K2 or flying solo to the North Pole. He disappeared floating down the Amazon or climbing the Andes or something. It was this big, tragic family secret no one ever talked about."

"So he just disappeared? They never found a body?" Kat said.

"No. Why?"

The train kept racing, but to Kat, everything was growing slow and still. She felt it in the crew around her, all gazes, all thoughts settling on her as she breathed against the chilly glass and whispered, "Anastasia."

2 DAYS UNTIL THE GALA

BROOKLYN, NEW YORK, USA

CHAPTER 27

For an odd sort of girl, Kat was used to odd sorts of meetings, but there was something especially strange about walking into Uncle Eddie's parlor and looking out over the people who sat straight-backed on the dusty, faded chairs.

"Hi." She shifted a little more nervously than someone of her pedigree ever should, and then she risked a glance at Hale, who stood beside her. "Thanks for coming, everybody. Have you all met?"

She looked from Marcus, Marianne, and Silas to the Bagshaws, Simon, and Gabrielle. Uncle Eddie stood by the fireplace, firmly in the center, and Kat had to wonder how she had ended up there, with these people for clients and crew.

"So everyone doing okay?" she asked. No one answered. "Okay."

"Did you find the will?" Marianne asked.

Kat smiled sadly. "No. I'm sorry, Marianne. We think any trace of Hazel's real will has probably been destroyed. But"—she hurried to add the good news—"if we can prove that Garrett stole from the company, we may be able to petition the courts to name a new trustee."

"I'll take care of you, Marianne," Hale told her. "I will always take care of you."

Marianne smiled and dabbed at a tear in her eye.

"Thanks to Silas," Kat went on, "we finally know what's going on. It looks like Garrett has stolen the Genesis prototype and its plans and is trying to sell them to one of Hale Industries' competitors. That's the bad news."

"Does that mean there's good news?" Silas asked.

"Sort of." Kat drew a deep breath. "We know where they are. Garrett has a safety deposit box at the Superior Bank of Manhattan, and we're pretty sure the prototype and plans are in there."

Kat saw her uncle tense, but he didn't speak. She could read his eyes: *That is hardly good news.*

"It is an extremely difficult target. No one has ever robbed it. Ever. And we can't do a job like that in time for the launch. We may never be able to do it, and so that's why, Silas, we need you working to duplicate the prototype. Can you do that?"

"I can try," Silas said. "But without access to my lab and—"

"I'll get you whatever you need," Hale said.

"Good," Kat told him. "Simon can help you try to recover the original schematics from the Hale Industries server."

"That's very nice," Silas said with a smile. "But I've been

working with that system since before he was born, and I haven't—"

"I think you'll find that Simon's skill set is slightly more . . . specific," Kat said.

"I steal things," Simon told him.

Silas arched an eyebrow. "I see," he said, then crossed his arms and grinned in the manner of a man who can't wait to get to work.

"Great. So while Silas is trying to duplicate the prototype, we'll try to retrieve the original."

"Retrieve?" Marianne asked.

"Steal," Gabrielle and the Bagshaws said in unison.

"Oh." Marianne gave a sigh that said this day was getting more scandalous—and interesting—by the second.

"Now, forgive me for pointing out the obvious," Silas shifted in his chair and leaned closer to Kat, "but retrieving the original isn't going to do us any good after Garrett rolls out the fake at the gala two nights from now."

"That's why we're going to disrupt the launch," she said.

"You know," Angus said, "I've got a little C-four that I've been saving for a rainy—"

"We're not blowing up my company, Angus," Hale said.

"Righto. Carry on, Kitty."

"Like I was saying, we're going to have to disrupt the launch, hopefully in a way that will keep it from being rescheduled any time soon. Also, we need to keep Garrett . . . distracted."

The older generation sat looking at the younger, and Kat wondered exactly when and how the baton had been passed. She wanted to know if it was too late to give it back.

189

"And that's why"—she took a deep breath—"we're going to run a con. It hasn't been done in a long time, but that's okay, because we have the talent to pull it off." She felt her hands shake, so she gripped one in the other. "Have you ever heard the story of the Grand Duchess Anastasia?"

"Well, of course," Marcus said. "She was Russian royalty, killed in the uprising. Now, some people said that she had survived, but that was a conspiracy. A . . ."

"Con," Hale filled in.

Silas was shaking his head. "But what does this have to do with—"

"Reginald." Marianne's voice was solid and sure. "It is because of Reginald, isn't it? But . . . how? Who could possibly . . ." She let the words trail off, and Kat felt the room shift, all eyes turning to Uncle Eddie.

"No." Eddie was starting toward the kitchen. "No," he said again, once Kat had caught up to him. He was trying to act normal—like he wasn't upset—but he went to his stove and began moving pots from burner to burner, and Kat thought that, for one of the world's greatest bluffers, it was a shame for him to have such an obvious tell.

"You're the only one who can do it, Uncle Eddie."

"No, Katarina," he said. "No man alive can do it."

"We have to try. It doesn't have to be the full Anastasia, just enough to delay a few days. All we need to do is keep Garrett too busy to prove that the Hales have a fake, and appease his buyer. We do that and then—"

"It cannot be done." It was more proclamation than statement, the lord high grifter telling all who could hear that the Anastasia was dead.

"Yes, it can be. *You* can do it."

"I could have," he admitted. "Maybe. If it were thirty years ago and I were ten years younger. But the Anastasia is not an easy thing, Katarina. It is a dead con."

"So no one will be expecting it."

"I'm saying it is impossible!"

His fist banged against the counter. The pots shook. All Kat could think was that she had never heard her uncle yell before. Not at her. Not in that room. He was the sort of man for whom a whisper carried far more force than a shout.

Then he took a deep breath and steadied his nerves. "With science—DNA—it cannot succeed."

"We don't need it to succeed. We just need it to buy us a little time."

"There is never going to be enough time to rob the Superior Bank of Manhattan."

Kat knew he was right, but she didn't dare say so. "So we'll buy enough time to find some other way. You can do this, Uncle Eddie." She eased closer, placed her hand on top of his. "Please."

"You are a smart girl, Katarina. But young. I think this time you are not thinking with your head," Eddie told her. "Someday you will know that the heart is not always as wise as it is strong."

"Uncle Eddie . . ." Kat's voice broke. She was too busy thinking about the files in Garrett's office, wondering just how many secrets had once lain inside the one labeled *Scooter*, and her hands began to tremble, knowing she'd just stolen Hale back. She didn't want to lose him again.

"Uncle Eddie," Hale said from the door.

The old man shifted his gaze to the boy, looked at him like he was an outsider, a stranger. A threat. Kat wondered how her life would have turned out if she'd left that fateful night two years before with a painting and not a boy.

"You still owe me for my window."

"Ten percent," Hale told him flatly. "I will give you ten percent of Hale Industries if you do this."

"Hale . . ." Kat said, dumbfounded.

"Okay," Hale countered before Eddie had even said a word. "Fifteen."

"You think I don't want to do this because there's nothing in it for me?"

"I think you're the greatest thief in the world. And without you—in a month—Hale Industries will be half as valuable as it is today, so that's why I'm willing to give you *twenty* percent of a billion-dollar corporation for a week's worth of work."

Kat stood quietly, honestly not sure what would happen next. Hale sounded like himself. He looked perfectly normal. But there was something there, a raw, aching thread, and Kat knew that if she pulled it, his whole world might unravel.

"Please, Uncle Eddie." She pleaded with the only man who could fix it all, watched him sink carefully into a chair. He moved like every bone in his body was threatening to break, and Kat half expected to hear a creak as he placed his elbows on the table.

"Your mother brought a strange man to this house once, Katarina. I had hoped it might be a few more years before history repeated itself."

Kat rolled her eyes at the mention of her father. "Uncle Eddie, I brought Hale home ages ago," she reminded him; but her uncle just shook his head.

"I've known my great-niece's friend. A boyfriend, on the other hand . . . that is a most different matter."

"Yes, sir," Hale said. He stood up a little straighter, spoke a little louder.

"You have a powerful family, boy."

"Yes, sir," Hale said. "Please don't hold them against me."

Then Eddie gave a wry smile. "Who says I was talking about *them*?"

ONE DAY BEFORE
THE GALA

SOMEWHERE
IN NEW JERSEY

CHAPTER 28

The abandoned lab they rented was somewhere in New Jersey. Gabrielle drove while Kat's mind drifted, nothing but a massive list of all the things she had to do. So when they finally walked through the main doors, her first thought was that they must have been in the wrong place.

The only light came through grit-covered windows. A thick layer of dust covered everything: crates and shelves and long rows of tarp-covered equipment.

But then there were the voices. Kat followed them through a maze of crates bearing the Hale Industries logo until she could see Marcus in the center of a wide empty room, pacing. He had a ruler in his hand, and when he stopped, he looked at Eddie, who sat in the center of the space on an old office chair.

"The Hale men have all graduated from which academy?" Marcus asked.

"Colgan." Eddie glared at Hale. "And I believe that is all Hale men but *one*."

"Correct," Marcus said, and kept on pacing. "As a child, Reginald had three nannies, all named . . ."

"Beatrice," Eddie said.

"But he called them . . ."

"Bunny," Eddie replied with a cringe.

"Correct. In an interview with *Esquire* magazine, Reginald listed his interests as . . ."

"Polo and sailing," Eddie said.

"But his actual pastimes were . . ."

"Drinking and womanizing," Eddie replied.

"Correct." Marcus gave a nod and studied his pupil, while Kat skirted the edge of the room and took a seat next to Hale.

"How's it going?" she whispered.

"Okay. I think. To be honest, I'm not really sure. Marcus is acting . . . scary."

"Posture!" Marcus snapped. "Hale men do not slouch."

"Yeah," Kat said. "He is."

Then it was Marianne's turn to look Eddie up and down. She spoke to her brother. "Marcus, if I'm to be honest, I'm more concerned about his *overall* presence. Edward can memorize all the facts we give him, I'm certain. But Reginald had such vigor—such spirit. His manner was very distinctive."

"True," Marcus said.

"Let me see you walk," Marianne told Eddie, who stood and took a few steps across the floor.

Marcus eyed Eddie from a new perspective. "The shoulders are off."

"His hands are wrong," Marianne said as if Eddie wasn't even there.

"Don't forget the limp," Marcus told Eddie.

Kat looked at Hale. "I've never heard Marcus talk this much."

"Yeah," Hale whispered. "I'm trying to decide if I like it."

Just then, Marcus took the ruler and struck Eddie in the stomach. "Hale men speak from the diaphragm!"

Hale nodded. "I definitely like it."

Kat leaned her elbows on the table, and for the first time, noticed the piles that were collected there.

Old family albums lay spread across the surface. Black-and-white photos had been pulled from the pages, and Kat flipped through them one by one, staring down at the face of the same young man. Tall and strong and golden.

Standing among a tribe in Kenya, a lion at his feet. Posing with a team of dogs in the blowing snow at the top of the world. On a raft in the Amazon. Climbing K2.

Kat looked from the young man in the picture to the boy who sat beside her, and she wondered if trying to steal a more exciting life might be at least a little bit genetic.

"Here," Marianne said. "Watch this. See the way Reginald carries himself?"

Suddenly, the lights went out and the beam of a projector was slicing through the room, splashing across a white wall, beneath high, dingy windows. Watching, Kat forgot what century—much less what year—they were in, because on the screen it was the Hamptons in summer. There were girls in tennis whites and men in seersucker suits. Slowly, the camera panned across a wide lawn, taking in the smiling faces and waving hands. There was an undeniable resemblance among them all, and Kat, who had a long line of "relatives" who didn't share the same blood, had to remind herself that there are some families that do have the same smile—the same eyes.

Then she remembered why they seemed so familiar, and she turned to take in the boy beside her. But it was like Hale had forgotten she was there. He was staring at the flickering image, being pulled into a memory that wasn't his own.

"That's her," he whispered.

"Who?" Kat asked.

He pointed. "Hazel. That's her."

There were three young women on the screen, but one stood apart from the group. She kept her hands intertwined, like someone who had been invited—but not born—inside the family.

Kat watched her smile and laugh. The wind blew through her hair, and it was easy for Kat to imagine the cool breeze and warm sun on the woman's skin, but she wasn't truly comfortable there on that sunny stretch of lawn.

"Which one is Reginald?" Kat pointed back to the screen.

"In the hat," Hale said just as, in the video, the long-lost uncle slapped the recently departed grandmother on the butt.

"See," Marianne told Eddie. "Vigor!"

"Yes, Edward," Marcus agreed. "Do you think you can capture that?"

But Kat didn't listen for the answer. She was too entranced by the woman on the screen. "She was beautiful."

Hale tilted his head. "She was lonely."

Kat knew that he was right. She was also certain that he knew the feeling. The Hale name was his birthright and legacy, but like his grandmother, he had never truly belonged.

Kat watched Hale's face change and knew that the sadness

he had carried since the funeral was back. He wasn't okay. She saw it in him, lingering just under the surface, waiting to break free.

There were flash cards with photos of distant relatives, a quiz about the family pets. Kat had been by Hale's side almost constantly for over two years, but she learned more about his family in those four hours than she had ever even suspected before. And through it all, Eddie never wavered or complained, soaking up the facts and figures like a sponge.

"And when they ask for a DNA test?" Marianne asked at last. Kat could tell the question had been weighing on her for hours, and finally she couldn't hold it back anymore. "What will we do then?"

Kat thought about her uncle's words, his warnings. He was right, of course. The Anastasia was a dead con, but they didn't have to steal the company. She smiled. They only had to steal time.

"Simple, Marianne. We stall," Kat said.

"I know Garrett, child," Marianne said. "I've known him since he was no older than you. And, believe me, if that man wants something, it will be quite hard to stop him."

Hale took her hand. "Marianne, can you trust me?"

"Of course," she said. Then a strange look crossed her face.

"What is it?" Hale asked.

"I just keep thinking that if your grandmother were here now . . ."

"She'd be pretty disappointed, huh?" Hale asked, head down.

"No." Marianne took his face in her hands. "She'd be having a fabulous time."

For the first time in days, Hale smiled, and a sharp feeling shot through Kat, the possibility that maybe he might come back to her. That maybe, just maybe, Hale might not be entirely gone.

"Okay, we have work to do," Eddie said, shuffling toward them. He turned to Kat. "Shouldn't you be casing a bank?"

"I have my best people on it."

"I wouldn't call Angus and Hamish your best," Eddie said. "But they'll do. And you." He pointed at Hale. "Isn't it time you went home?"

Home. It was easy for Kat to forget that Hale had one when, in fact, he had several.

"Oh," Hale said. "Right. See you at the gala?" he asked.

"I wouldn't miss it," Kat said. She watched Hale move into the shadows of the building, nothing but footsteps retreating, beating out a pulse somewhere deep inside of Kat, telling her it was too late to stop now.

DAY OF
THE LAUNCH

BROOKLYN, NEW YORK,
USA

CHAPTER 29

Katarina Bishop didn't like dresses. It wasn't a feminist statement. She would never judge anyone who felt the call of a twirly skirt or toile-covered confections. But once a girl gets a bow caught in a security gate at Buckingham Palace, it stands to reason that she would be a no-fuss, no-muss, jeans-and-T-shirt type of female. Unfortunately, it was not a jeans-and-T-shirt type of night.

"Stand still," Gabrielle told her. She squeezed the smaller girl by the shoulders and tugged on a string.

"Ouch," Kat said.

"You've got a little waist," Gabrielle said. "That's good. At least something's smaller than your boobs."

"Well," Kat said, "that's a relief."

Gabrielle shrugged. "Don't shoot the messenger."

"Shooting wasn't what I had in mind."

Kat wanted nothing more than to take off the gown and burn the high heels that Gabrielle had picked out for the occasion, but every thief knows that camouflage is half the battle, and Kat was standing on the brink of enemy territory. She needed all the help she could get.

"What kind of company has a black-tie-optional product launch?" Kat asked.

"The *Hale* kind," Gabrielle said, not looking up. "And it's not a launch, it's a *gala*. And from what I hear, it's going to be a huge homage to Hazel or something; so, even without the con, this is a big night for Hale. And you're going."

"Are you scolding me?" Kat asked. She had to wonder if this was what it felt like to be a teenage girl with a mother.

"I'm telling you that Kat-the-girlfriend has work to do. Tonight isn't just about Kat-the-thief."

"I know," Kat said.

Gabrielle stepped back and eyed her cousin. "Because you realize you just sent him back into the lion's den, don't you?"

Kat thought about the dark look that crossed his face every time he saw a picture of his grandmother, of the loneliness that lived behind those eyes, and said, "I know."

"With his family."

"*I know*," Kat said one final time.

"And old friends . . ." Gabrielle didn't finish the thought. She just looked Kat up and down. "I bet Natalie's wearing heels tonight."

"Good for her."

"Come on, Kat."

"I'm not worried Hale's going to cheat, Gabrielle." Kat studied her reflection in the mirror. "I'm just . . ."

Gabrielle took a step back, but she wasn't looking at Kat's dress or her hair. She stared squarely into her cousin's eyes and said, "Spill."

"I'm not sure. It's just . . . Do you think he's doing okay?"

Gabrielle considered the question, and when she answered, she spoke carefully, like the words themselves might easily bruise. "I don't know, Kat. I really don't. I'm lucky. I've never lost anyone. But I am curious—two weeks after your mother died, how were you?"

Kat stared into the mirror and tried hard not to think about the answer.

CHAPTER 30

Whe Kat, at last, saw the main entrance of Hale Industries, the lobby was filled with towering arrangements of flowers on every table, an orchestra playing near the stairs. But walking through the door with Gabrielle, Kat looked around at the people who filled the party, all decked out in their finest gems, and she realized she'd rather be in the alley with Silas than at the party with these people any day.

She was, however, alone in that opinion.

"Ooh," Gabrielle said when a woman walked past in a diamond and emerald choker. "I want it."

"No," Kat said.

"But did you see the clasp? A simple Bump and Dump will—"

"No more emeralds," Kat said.

Gabrielle stopped short and nodded. "Right. Good point. No more emeralds."

Suddenly, Kat couldn't stand still. Her fingers drummed against her hips, and she shifted her feet from side to side. She would have given anything to stop moving. Or, better yet, to go back to the lab and ask Silas for the millionth time if he was making any progress. They needed that prototype, and they were going to need it soon.

"Stop fidgeting," Gabrielle spat. "You look like you're up to something sketchy."

"We *are* up to something sketchy," Kat spat back.

"Technicality," Gabrielle said with a wave, and Kat took a deep breath and tried to scan the room while her cousin started to walk away, calling over her shoulder one last time. "It's showtime."

Kat recognized some of Hale's family members from the funeral. On the other side of the crowd she could see Garrett's assistant chatting with a member of the board. There were journalists and society mavens, a party crasher or two. But on the far side of the room, between the curving stairs that led to the second story, stood a stage, and on that stage stood a portrait of Hazel and a very faulty prototype beneath a velvet curtain.

Kat was half tempted to charge across the room and storm the stage, grab the prototype, and disappear. But before she could even move, she saw Garrett appear at the top of the stairs. He lingered there, studying the crowd that filled the grand space below, a wry smile on his lips. He looked very much like a man who had bet against the house. And won.

It was a shame he didn't notice when Gabrielle walked up behind him. She stumbled slightly, and he caught her. He never even felt the tiny bug she attached to the face of his wristwatch.

"Done?" Kat asked when Gabrielle returned to her side.

Her cousin looked offended. "Of course."

A moment later, Simon's voice was in Kat's ear, saying, "Kat, the bug is working. I've just got to . . ."

Simon's voice trailed off as though he were lost in thought, while another man made his way toward where Garrett stood on the staircase.

"Looks like our friend from Hong Kong made it," Gabrielle said, then jerked upright and stared at Kat, wide-eyed. "You don't think Garrett's going to sell the prototype tonight, do you?"

"Come on, Simon," Kat said.

"Just a second," Simon chided back, but the man from Hong Kong was already walking away, and Kat was just starting to relax, to think maybe they would make it, when a woman brushed against her in the crowd. She cut Gabrielle off—actually caused her to stumble—before making her way toward the trustee.

"Who does she think she is?" Gabrielle asked, pouting at the only woman in the room who was possibly as beautiful as she was. Together, she and Kat stood watching as the woman strolled toward Garrett and tapped him on the shoulder.

He smiled like a man completely unaccustomed to the attention of a gorgeous woman, but neither Kat nor Gabrielle could hear a word of their conversation.

"Simon," Kat asked. "Where's that audio?"

A second later, Simon must have flipped a switch, because the lawyer's voice was booming into their ears.

"Hello," he said, extending a hand. "Ms. . . ."

210

"Montenegro." The woman spoke English with a heavy French accent. "I was hoping to meet you here, Mr. Garrett. When I saw you speaking with our Hong Kong competitor, you had me quite worried. Please tell me I'm not too late."

"I'm afraid I don't know what you mean," Garrett huffed and started to turn away, but the woman was having none of it.

"Of course you do." She gave a beguiling smile. "It would be a great pity if Genesis were to find a new home without first considering *all* the possibilities."

"My dear woman, we are here to celebrate the life of Hazel Hale and the launch of Genesis."

"Yes." She looked around the room. "Either that or we are here to prove to all interested parties that the Hale model will not be in production for at least nine months. Maybe longer." She pulled a flute of champagne from a passing tray, then scanned the crowd. "And let me just say that I represent a *very* interested party."

This, at last, seemed to catch Garrett's attention. "Is that so?"

"It is. What if I were to say that my employer is prepared to take the prototype off your hands as early as . . . say . . . the day after tomorrow?"

"I'd say that two weeks is a very short time to wait for a very big reward."

"Why wait two weeks when we could conclude our business so much sooner?"

"Once we prove the Hale model is defective, I have a buyer who is willing to pay full market value for Genesis—not *black market* value. There's a difference, Ms. Montenegro. And the difference is worth two weeks of waiting."

"Oh. What a pity." Then one elegant hand reached to smooth his lapel and slip a business card into his pocket. "My number," she said. "For when you change your mind."

When Kat watched her walk away, the clock that had been running inside her head began to tick louder and louder until she thought her mind might explode.

"Gabrielle?" Kat swallowed hard. "How soon do you think we can rob the Superior Bank of Manhattan?"

Walking through the party, Kat couldn't help but think that she really didn't have time for a party. She had things to do, places to see. Prototypes to steal. She was just starting to plan her escape when she heard her name shouted through the crowd.

"Kat!" Natalie screamed and threw out her arms, pulled Kat into a massive bear hug, and Kat remembered why she wasn't friends with many girls. She was a lot of things, after all, but *hugger* wasn't one of them.

"Hi, Natalie," Kat said, prying herself away. "It's nice to see you."

The girl stumbled a little, listing like a boat on uneven waters, and Kat knew something was wrong.

"Natalie, are you okay?"

"Kat!" Natalie tried to whisper, but failed. "Can you keep a secret?"

"Yeah," Kat said. "I think I can."

"We got into the liquor cabinet."

"Natalie . . ." Kat said, letting the word draw out. "Who is *we*?"

Natalie hiccuped, pulled a hand guiltily to her face, and smiled. "Who knew Scooter could pick a lock?"

Kat's blood went cold. "I did."

She wanted it to be part of the con, a trick. But it wasn't, Kat was sure. She thought about the sad, lonely boy looking at his family's photos, and she cursed herself for not predicting that something like this was bound to happen.

"Kat?" Natalie whispered again. "Kat, what's wrong?"

But Kat was already shaking her head and pushing away, saying, "Sorry, Nat. I've got to . . . go."

Kat wheeled, searching the crowd for Gabrielle. Then her gaze drifted to the boy who was already halfway down the sweeping stairs, in something between a walk and a jog, looking like he was a top hat away from giving Fred Astaire a run for his money.

"Oh, Kat!" Hale's mother cried out. "Kat, darling, come over here. There are some people I'd love for you to—"

"I'm sorry. I've got to . . ." But Kat couldn't finish. She was too busy pushing through the crowd, almost willing Hale to catch her eye, give a wink, a smile. She thought that surely he would find some way to see her—just her. But he didn't.

"Where is he going?" Kat asked when she finally reached Gabrielle.

"I don't know," Gabrielle said. "Ooh. Shrimp." She reached for the tray of a passing waiter, but Kat caught her arm.

"Gabrielle, Hale's not right. We've got to stop him. I think he might be . . ."

But then Hale stumbled, climbing up onto the stage that held the prototype, and Gabrielle finished for her.

"Drunk."

The lights went out. A spotlight shone on the stage and the boy the family knew as Scooter. A hush fell over the crowd as he took up the microphone and began to speak.

"I'd like to thank everyone for coming. It's a very special night, and we're all here to celebrate a very special woman. My grandmother." Hale pointed to the oil portrait that had been moved from the upstairs corridor and placed at the corner of the stage. A polite smattering of applause went through the crowd.

Kat couldn't move. A dozen different scenarios played out in her mind, but Hale was like a runaway train, and she had no idea how to find the brakes.

"My grandmother loved Genesis!" Hale threw up his hands as if expecting the well-heeled crowd to erupt into thunderous applause. "They wanted me to tell you all about Genesis. It's the future of the company, they say. *It. And me.* Some future, huh?" Hale said, and the forced chuckles morphed into sighs of disbelief. "I'm glad she's dead. I'm glad she's not here to see this."

"Kat," Gabrielle whispered, "do we stop him? Kat, what do we do?"

But Kat didn't know. She hadn't planned for this scenario, and a part of her was too busy cursing herself for that to do anything else. "He wasn't ready," she mumbled. "He wasn't—"

"Scooter." Hale's father stepped into the spotlight and reached for his son's arm. "Scooter, that's enough."

"My name's not Scooter!" Hale yelled, revolting and pulling away. "My name is . . ." But he trailed off, and Kat could have sworn she finally caught his gaze. "I guess it doesn't matter what you call me. It's never mattered. I'm *a HALE.*"

More than before, he slurred his words.

"I'm *the* Hale," he went on. "Or so they tell me. The great hope—the heir apparent. The—"

"I'm sorry, young man, but I'm going to have to disagree with that."

An older man was climbing onto the stage, stepping into the light. He didn't look like Hale or his father. The overcoat was a little too out of date. He leaned too heavily on his cane, as if it weren't a mere walking stick but a crutch with actual purpose. But when he spoke, there was no mistaking he was an important man, a formidable figure.

A member of the family.

"Hello, Junior," he said to Hale's father. "Don't you have a hug for your favorite uncle?"

CHAPTER 31

The man on the stage had wild white hair and wore a secondhand suit. The cane was rough and wooden, and his tie hadn't been in style for thirty years. He was a relic. A drifter. But there was something about him—a power so strong and ancient that it was almost like the man had been forged out of cast iron. He was an unmovable force, and it would take more than a scene to make him leave.

"Well, I was told this was where the party was!" he yelled at the crowd and continued across the stage—past Hale and his father, to the portrait of the woman of the hour.

Even knowing what she knew, Kat had a hard time seeing her uncle in the man at the front of the room. Everything was different. He leaned heavily on his cane and took slow, careful

216

steps until he finally reached the portrait. Then he bent down and brushed a kiss across Hale's grandmother's painted cheek.

"I told you I'd come home, Hazel," he told the painting. "I'm just a little late."

He reached up as if to trace a finger against the face on the portrait, but Hale's father caught his hand.

"Don't touch that," Senior spat.

"Well, it doesn't compare to the original, but it will do."

"You knew her?" Hale's father asked.

Eddie smiled. "Of course I knew her. She was married to my brother."

"He's gonna blow it," Kat said.

"He's fine," Gabrielle assured her.

"He's not ready," Kat said.

"He was born ready," Gabrielle retorted.

"He's not—"

On the stage, Hale's father said, "But that would make you . . ."

"Junior," Eddie said with a scowl, "you got old."

"It's Senior now," Hale's father spat. "Now I demand to know the meaning of this! My uncle Reginald is dead, and you're nothing but an imposter. Get out of my building."

"Actually, I'm not an imposter." A thought seemed to occur to Uncle Eddie. "Which, I believe, makes this *my* building." He gave a hearty laugh.

"I don't believe it," Senior said. "It can't be. You cannot be—"

"Reginald?" Marianne's voice was shaking. "Reginald, is that you?"

She looked beautiful, Kat couldn't help but think. She

wore a long black gown, and her gray hair was piled elegantly onto the top of her head. But it wasn't just her clothing that had changed. There was a confidence, a grace about her as she said, "Reginald, it *is* you."

The words were breathless, hopeful. She didn't look like someone who had a seen a ghost. She sounded like someone lost in a dream.

"Hello, Marianne." Eddie lingered on the word, then kissed her cheek. "You're looking well, my dear."

He gave her a sly wink, and when he pinched the maid's bottom, Kat heard Hale's aunt tell her husband, "Well, he certainly *acts* like Reginald."

Then Eddie turned his attention to Hale. "So, I assume that you're the young man who inherited Hazel's half of the company."

Only Garrett was able to speak. "Her . . . half?"

But Eddie didn't bother to respond. He just kept studying Hale.

"Looks like you need to learn to hold your liquor." Then he gave Hale a hard slap on the back and let out a loud, raucous laugh. "Who better to help you with that than me?"

"I don't believe it." Hale's father was shaking his head. "I don't believe you. Where have you been for fifty years? If you're Reginald Hale, where did you go?"

Uncle Eddie smiled. There was a sparkle in his eyes, a glimmer. "Oh, that's easy, Junior. I went crazy."

For a groundbreaking piece of technology, Genesis was easily forgotten. Reporters yelled their questions for the old man, the new toy still covered with its cloth, shrouded in secrecy until another day. The catastrophe was averted and the spotlight had shifted, and Kat tried to savor the moment.

But then her cousin bumped her shoulder.

"Congratulations, Kat," Gabrielle said. "He's in. Of course, you know what this means. . . ."

"We're going to need a Big Store," Kat guessed.

Gabrielle nodded slowly. "We're going to need a Big Store."

Who had used the phrase *Big Store* first, Kat had to wonder as she walked toward Hale Industries' back doors, looking forward to the short cab ride home. It didn't really matter. In her head, lists were forming, phone numbers were swirling, and above it all, a clock was ticking down, second by second, toward Genesis's imminent sale.

Two weeks. But maybe less. Maybe the Hong Kong buyer would back out now that the Hale demo had been upstaged. Maybe Garrett would give Ms. Montenegro a call and shift the time frame altogether. But Kat wasn't a girl who was used to banking on maybes. There was a date on the calendar and it was circled in red, and Kat knew that eventually she was going to have to retrieve the prototype from the bank across the street.

When she reached the back doors she'd first used with Silas, Kat stopped and stared through the narrow windows at the bank, just fifteen feet away. Even without looking, she would have known what was there.

Steel and iron and the best cameras and guards that money could buy. A vault five stories beneath one of the most crowded streets on earth, in a place where nothing ever went unnoticed.

But Kat was going to get that prototype. Either she was going to steal it or Silas was going to remake it. She didn't know how, but she knew she would get her hands on it eventually. She had to.

"Did you have fun tonight, Miss Bishop?"

Kat turned at the sound of the voice. Garrett was walking toward her. He kept his hands in his pockets, and his gaze locked on hers.

"It was lovely," Kat said.

"That was quite a surprise, wasn't it?" He ambled closer. Kat felt the cool glass of the window against her back. "Your boyfriend's long-lost great-uncle showing up like that . . ."

"Yes." Kat forced a little laugh. "I figured they probably needed some family time, so I was just going to—"

"But you know all about great-uncles, don't you, Katarina?"

"I—"

"No lies, Kat." Garrett's chest rose and fell too quickly. Kat thought for a moment he might collapse, that maybe his heart was giving out. "Show me at least a little respect."

"I don't know what you mean," Kat said.

"Oh, I think you do, because, you see, I know who you are." His breath was acrid and hot on her cheek. He brushed a finger down the side of her face until his hand rested on her throat. He squeezed gently at first. Then harder. "And I know *what* you are."

"Let me go." Kat's voice quivered. The party was still in full swing at the end of the hall, and Kat grappled for options. "I'll yell. I'll tell security."

"No. You won't. I don't think your kind of criminal ever actually *calls* the authorities."

"I don't know what you're talking about." Kat tried to pull his hand off of her throat, push herself past him; but his other hand flew over her head, crashing into the door and holding it solidly in place.

"I said," he spoke slowly, "show me some respect."

Trembling, Kat watched the way the sweat gathered at his brow, his face red and flushed, as he fumed like an animal that was cornered and beginning to fight. He's desperate, Kat thought. Then, just that quickly, she realized, *No, he's dangerous.*

"What?" he asked, then bit back an evil, bitter laugh. "Did you honestly believe that no one in Scooter's life knew where he was going—what he was doing? Didn't you ever wonder why no member of the Hale family ever asked or cared when the golden boy was halfway around the world . . . with you?"

"I know my boyfriend from school," Kat said. But again the man laughed.

"I thought you'd be a much better liar. Aren't all thieves liars? Isn't that how you stole the Cleopatra Emerald? Was that fun for you? It looked like fun from where I was standing."

Kat thought about the empty file labeled *Scooter* and finally knew what had lain inside it. They weren't Hale's secrets. They were hers. And this man seemed to know every one.

"What do you want with me?"

He let go of her neck, but didn't leave.

"Don't think you've won this game, Kat. Do not make the mistake of believing that I haven't seen you and your family's interference coming from a mile away. Of course, 'Uncle Reginald' "—he held up his fingers and made mock quotations around the words—"was a nice touch. Some might even say inspired. But I will win, Miss Bishop. In fact, I have already won. You just can't see it yet."

"No. *You* can't see," Kat told him. "You're going to lose."

He was bigger, stronger, crazier, but that didn't matter. Not right then. Because Kat finally had the home court advantage, and she felt a new kind of strength rushing through her. All pretense was gone. She didn't have to lie, to pretend she was anything other than a seasoned thief talking to a newcomer to the game.

Garrett looked across the alley.

"It can be done," Kat said, reading his mind, knowing he was thinking about the bank that had never been robbed. She whispered, "And I'm going to do it."

"Oh, watch what you say, Kat. It would be a shame if everything I knew were to find its way to . . . say . . . the Henley."

He reached to tuck a stray piece of hair behind her ear, and Kat trembled. She remembered the look on Arturo Taccone's face as the gangster threatened everyone she'd ever loved; the smile the grifter called Maggie had given her when locking Kat inside a tiny room. She'd seen a lot of very bad people up close in her short life, but there was something about Garrett in that moment that scared her. Greed had made him crazy and reckless, and he was going to take Kat down with him.

"I have cleaned up my last Hale family mess, Miss Bishop. You and your little boyfriend are on your own as far as I'm concerned." He laughed again. "Let's see how far you make it now."

"What's that supposed to mean?" Kat blurted, but the man simply turned.

"You'll see, my dear. You will see."

13 DAYS UNTIL THE SALE

VENICE, ITALY

CHAPTER 32

Over the course of the next twelve hours, Kat made twenty-one phone calls to six different continents. (Uncle Lester was doing a job off the coast of Antarctica and was very adamant that he not be disturbed for any reason.)

There was Uncle Sal in Rio; the Johnson twins, who were out on parole near Sydney. She personally composed a telegram for Uncle Marco (his preferred method of communication) and left a note in a dead letter drop for Uncle Felix, who had sworn off telephones after a particularly nasty MI5 experience in '92.

But there was one member of the family for whom no call or note or message would do, so that was how Kat found herself in Venice.

Spring had already come to St. Mark's Square as Kat

walked alone that morning. Warm breezes blew off the Mediterranean, carrying tourists from cruise ships and exotic ports of call. But Kat couldn't let herself be distracted, not by the high-end boutiques that lined the narrow alleys, not even by the smell of pasta or massive displays of fresh fruit that filled the stalls of the open-air markets. She wasn't there as a tourist, and yet she was far from a native. So Kat walked into the cathedral, trying to find some peace.

Venice was sinking—everybody knew it. The tiles on the floor of St. Mark's Cathedral rose and fell like the waves in the bay, unwilling to give up without a fight. Overhead, a beautiful mosaic of apostles and saints smiled down. It was a house of miracles, so Kat said a silent prayer, needing one of her own.

A group of tourists passed by, snapping pictures, and Kat stood silently, taking it all in. She saw a man leaving the confessional, his dark robes billowing behind him as he walked, and she chased after him.

He was already in the square when she summoned her courage and yelled, "Father!"

The priest stopped and turned, then smiled when Kat said, "Hi, Daddy."

"So it's true." He draped an arm around her shoulder as they walked. "My baby girl is setting up her first Big Store. You're growing up."

"What can I say? It was this or a Sweet Sixteen. I've always been sentimental." She leaned back and gave his robes a once-over. "Maybe I shouldn't walk so close to you. I don't want to get hit by lightning."

"Hey, don't blame me," her father told her. "I'm not the one who built a jewelry store behind a cathedral."

She couldn't deny he had a point.

"So"—Bobby gave her shoulder a squeeze—"I assume you've spoken to Uncle Felix?"

"He's in."

"What about Irina?"

Kat shrugged at the sound of Gabrielle's mother's name. "She's already working on something."

"Ezra?"

"He's the one who told me how to find you."

Bobby stopped short. Kat, not expecting that, walked past him a little, and had to stare back into the sun when he said, "You can always find me, Kat."

"I know."

"So are you going to tell me what's really wrong?"

Was he able to see through her so easily because he was a great grifter or a terrific father? Kat couldn't really tell. But that was just as well. It didn't really matter.

They walked together down the crumbling, sinking sidewalks of Venice, and Kat took a deep breath. "Hale needs your help, Daddy."

"Oh, *Hale* does, does he?" her father asked, then went on before she had the chance to answer. "What is the job?"

"We've got to do the Anastasia."

Bobby gave a deep whole-body laugh, then suddenly stopped. "You aren't serious. . . . Wait. Are you serious?" he asked, like she must be trying to con him.

She pulled a copy of the *Times* from her bag, pointed to a headline about the return of the long-lost Reginald Hale, and said, "We are. Uncle Eddie's already inside."

From the look that came next, Kat couldn't tell if her dad was proud or scared, or possibly a little of both.

"How'd you talk him into this?" Bobby shook the paper at Kat, pointing to the blurry picture of the old man with the cane.

"He's a man who appreciates family."

"And a share of the Hale family fortune?" Bobby guessed.

"That's not it." Kat tried and failed to pull the paper from her father's grasp.

"Oh," Bobby said as he slipped the paper under one arm, "I bet that's a little bit it."

The thought had crossed Kat's mind, of course. But this wasn't the time to linger on it.

"We need you, Dad."

"And by *we*, you mean . . ."

"Hale and I need you," Kat grudgingly admitted.

"So the rumors are true. . . . It's 'Hale and I' now, is it?"

"Hale's my best friend."

"He's a little more than that, from what I hear."

"Dad . . ." Kat said. "He's Hale. You know Hale."

"Oh, I know Hale. Once upon a time I *was* Hale." He studied her, then smiled. "I bet your Uncle Eddie is over the moon about this. He just loves it when his nieces bring boys home." He sounded as if at least a little part of Kat's new romantic status was giving him some pleasure. But not much.

"Dad . . ."

"And I should help my daughter's boyfriend because . . ."

"Technically, you still owe him for Taipei."

"Taipei was an exception. Taipei has no business being brought up in relation to—"

"He needs me, Dad." Kat let her gaze drift across the square. Her voice was soft as she finished, "He needs . . . us."

"What's wrong, Kat?" Bobby asked. He'd seen through

228

her, past her own personal guards and walls to the frightened girl who lived inside the seasoned thief's tough exterior.

"He's . . . different. Hale's different."

"He's a boy, Kat. I hate to break it to you, but we are fundamentally different."

"That's not it," she said. "It's like . . . I can feel him slipping away. Like the other night when he got drunk at the launch and—"

"Hale was drunk on the job? I'll kill him."

"I don't want him dead, Dad. I want him back."

"I thought you two were . . . together." The words sounded like they pained him, but Bobby said them anyway.

"We are. It's just . . . he's so sad. And so alone. It's like . . . I think he feels like I felt when we lost Mom."

"Then we'll get him back." Her father pulled her tightly toward him, placed a kiss on the top of her head. "We'll steal him if we have to."

"So you'll help me run my Big Store?" she asked, voice breaking, wiping tears from her eyes.

"Deal." Her father's arm fell gently around her shoulders.

"Oh." Kat stopped suddenly short. "There is one other thing."

"What?" Her father gave her that wide, easy smile—the one he never gave to marks and women, the one he saved just for her.

"After we set up the Big Store, I'm going to need you to help me rob the Superior Bank of Manhattan."

Bobby's jaw dropped. The cathedral bells chimed. Kat's father squeezed her shoulder tighter, and the two of them continued across the square.

"Oh, sweetheart, you are your mother's daughter."

"So you'll do it?"

"Yeah. But you're going to owe me."

There was a sidewalk café, and Kat stopped. "Fine. I'll buy you a cup of coffee."

He laughed. "Save your money, kiddo."

Kat pulled out a credit card that Hale had given her once for emergencies. "Then Hale can buy you a cup of coffee."

"Deal."

And in that moment, everything was okay. It was going to be fine, Kat thought as her father took his coffee, gave her a quick kiss on the forehead, and said, "See you in New York."

She watched him walk away, lost in thought. Planning. The pieces were right on the board in front of her. All she had to do was see what play Garrett was going to try next.

"*Signorina*, I'm sorry," the teller told her. "*Signorina*," the woman said again, pulling Kat's attention back to the café. "Your card," she said, reaching behind the counter for the largest, sharpest scissors that Kat had ever seen. "It is no good."

And then the woman cut, plastic pieces falling onto the counter, as Kat's mind drifted back to the crazed look in Garrett's eyes after the launch, the haunting threat that he was only just beginning to bring the fight to them.

Kat looked down at Hale's ruined card and muttered to herself, "Oh, boy."

12 DAYS BEFORE THE SALE

NEW YORK, NEW YORK, USA

CHAPTER 33

The penthouse on Park Avenue wasn't as grand as Hazel's country house. It was significantly less regal than the estate on the outskirts of London. But, walking through its shadowy halls, the one thing Kat knew for certain was that the more Hale family homes she saw, the more she understood why her boyfriend preferred the warmth of Uncle Eddie's kitchen.

"No one said I had a visitor," the figure on the other side of the bedroom doorway said.

Kat dangled a pair of needle-nose pliers and stepped into the well-appointed room. "Yeah, well. I didn't feel like bothering your parents. Besides, the new owner of Hale Industries deserves a top-rate security system. Figured I should test it."

"And?"

As soon as Hale stepped into the light, Kat knew he'd

been in bed. His hair was tousled and his shirt was off, and the smile he gave her was sleepy and lazy and warm.

"Doors and windows are top-notch, but the elevator shaft could use some work."

"I'll have my people get on that."

"Good," Kat said, and Hale smiled, and for a split second he was there—her Hale. He was laughing and biting back jokes. But just that quickly it was over, and he was the boy at the podium again, sad and lost and stumbling.

"So"—Hale looked down, ran a hand through his hair—"are you here to fire me or kill me?"

"Neither," Kat said. "You're not getting off that easily."

Hale dropped onto the corner of the bed. "I know."

Kat asked herself what Uncle Eddie would say, what her father might do. But Hale wasn't just a member of her crew who had messed up. He was Hale. Her Hale. And Kat just wanted him back. So she stepped a little closer and felt Hale's arms go around her waist.

"I'm so sorry, Kat." He pulled her tight. "I'm so, so sorry."

Kat had no choice but to run her hands through his hair. "Hale, look at me a second. I need to talk to you."

"Garrett cut me off. Credit cards, debit cards," Hale told her, then looked at her anew. "But you already know that, don't you?"

"I thought that might be the case when I couldn't pay for my dad's cup of coffee in Venice."

"You saw your dad?" Hale shot up. "What did you tell him?"

"Everything," Kat said, and Hale huffed, but Kat didn't let him stop her. "You honestly think he wasn't going to hear eventually? My family doesn't keep secrets, remember? Besides," she admitted, "we need him."

"Great. Now Bobby's going to hate me. More. Bobby's going to hate me *more*."

"Dad doesn't hate you. He just . . . well, Dad doesn't hate you any more than he would hate any boy who was . . . a boy."

"He doesn't hate the Bagshaws."

"The Bagshaws aren't boys. They are bombs with very colorful fuses."

"Good to know."

"So, has Garrett told your parents . . ."

"The truth about me?" Hale guessed. "Not yet. I rather imagine he doesn't want to explain where those Knightsbury tuition checks have been going all this time."

"True," Kat said, and nodded. "And he won't want to play all his cards quite yet."

And then something shifted inside of Hale. Kat watched it come over him like a shadow as he walked to the window and stared out at Central Park. He was older, wiser, and significantly richer than he'd been two years before, but right then Hale looked exactly like the boy who'd stood staring up at his first fake Monet.

"Will you still want me if I'm poor, Kat?"

"What kind of question is that?"

"No. Seriously. You're the planner. Simon's the genius. The Bagshaws are the muscle. And Gabrielle is . . . Gabrielle. But what am I, Kat? I'm the guy who writes the checks."

"No. You're the most naturally gifted inside man I have ever seen. And I was raised by Bobby Bishop." She made him look into her eyes. "I don't care about your money."

"What if we don't get it back, Kat? What if Genesis is gone?"

"Then we keep trying until we do get it back."

She wanted the words to work, to soothe, but Hale just shook his head.

"When I heard that my grandmother had left the company to me, I was . . . proud." He laughed a little. "I didn't want it. I didn't need it. I didn't really understand it . . . but it meant something to me."

"I know."

He moved closer. "I thought I was special. Turns out, I was just an easy mark."

"No," Kat snapped. She put her hands on his chest and felt the heat of his skin through her fingers. "If you don't want to be a victim, don't act like one."

It was fairly safe to assume that that was the first time anyone had ever spoken to W. W. Hale the Fifth in that manner. Kat was also fairly certain it wouldn't be the last.

"I might lose my grandmother's company."

Kat gave a smile and held Hale tight. "You won't lose me."

11 DAYS UNTIL THE SALE

BROOKLYN, NEW YORK, USA

CHAPTER 34

Kat had learned from a very young age never to be surprised by what she found in Uncle Eddie's kitchen. She'd seen it filled with exotic birds and black-market doctors treating dog bites, and at least once she'd walked in on Uncle Felix slipping into a dress and cursing the lack of women in their family.

But Kat had never seen the kitchen stunned before, and yet that was exactly the scene she found the next morning when she finally made her way downstairs.

"What do you mean Hale is out of money?" she heard Hamish asking as she walked down the hall. "Because, by 'out of money,' what you really mean is . . ."

"Is he going to have to give up the jet?" Angus asked.

"Boys." Kat's father's voice came floating toward her. "I just don't know."

"But—"

"Hamish." Kat rolled her eyes and shook her head, and they all turned sleepily toward where she was ladling herself a bowl of oatmeal. "He's *not* out of money. Or, not really out of money. Garrett has just cut off his credit cards. And his bank account. And taken most of his cash. And—"

"But the jet?" Angus asked a little wistfully.

Kat was just about to answer when another voice cut her off.

"I'm officially on the Hale Industries *Do Not Fly* list." Hale was there, standing in the doorway, and it felt to Kat like the room went even quieter. "So . . . hi, everyone."

There was Bobby and Eddie, both Bagshaws and Gabrielle. Marcus appeared behind Hale's shoulder, and his presence meant one thing: you simply cannot buy loyalty.

"So this is the young man who has intentions toward my little girl." Bobby shifted in his seat and crossed his legs.

"It is not so fun on this side of the table, is it, Robert?" Uncle Eddie huffed, and Kat had to remember that once upon a time her mother had been the dark-haired girl in that kitchen, and her dad had been the stray she'd brought home. She watched the two men looking at Hale as if they'd never before laid eyes on him.

"He's better-looking than the last vagabond I had to take in," Eddie said, standing and carrying empty bowls to the sink. "I'll give him that."

The insult slid off of Bobby like water. "So, you know, kid, according to thief culture, if you're going to court Kat, you now owe me two dozen goats."

"It's a dozen," Eddie corrected.

"Yeah, but Kat's worth two," Hamish said with a wink.

Through it all, Hale said nothing. Then, finally, he smiled. "I'm afraid I'm all out of goats at the moment, but I've got some ruby cuff links you can have."

"No." Bobby shook his head. "It's goats or nothing."

"Sorry, Kat." Hale shrugged, disappointed. "It was fun while it lasted."

"Don't look at me." Kat threw up her hands. "I'm officially ignoring all of you."

"Seriously, kid." Bobby extended a hand, and Hale took it. "I don't know whether to say congratulations or I'm sorry."

"Hazel was a great lady," Eddie added from the other side of the room.

"I wish I'd known her," Bobby said.

Hale flashed his easy grin. "You would have liked her. Everybody liked her the instant they met her. Isn't that right, Marcus?"

The butler stepped forward. "It is indeed, sir. Mrs. Hale was, if you'll pardon the term, a charmer."

"So she could have been an inside woman, huh?" Bobby asked.

"The best," Hale said, and for a second, that thought filled the room. Hale wasn't the boy who'd lost a fortune in that moment; he was the kid who'd lost his grandmother. And that made all the difference.

"So"—Bobby slapped the table—"I hear someone needs to rob the Superior Bank of Manhattan?"

"Yes, sir," Hale said.

Bobby pulled out a chair. "Have a seat."

How many times had Kat seen Hale at Eddie's kitchen

table? Too many to even count, she was sure. But right then she was holding her breath, hoping everything was going to be okay.

"Just to back up a moment. . . ." Hamish said. "So that I'm clear, we are supposed to run a dead con on someone who knows that we're conning him. . . ."

"Well, not him, exactly—my family," Hale said. "But pretty much. Go on."

"And we're supposed to set up a Big Store with no money," Hamish said.

"And rob the Superior Bank of Manhattan with no time," Angus finished.

"And then break into the U.S. Patent office to swap out the fake plans for the real plans. . . ." Hamish said. "Or something like that."

Kat looked around the room. If she could have chosen any crew in the world, it would have been them, but she didn't feel any peace.

"You're right, Hamish, I don't have any money," Hale said. "But I have some things we can sell."

"No, sir," Marcus chimed in. "I have savings, which I will happily contribute to—"

"No!" Eddie's fist banged against the table. "You think this is supposed to be easy? In my day we had to work for what we stole. We didn't fly around on private jets. No one wrote us a check and bought us a Big Store. We made our own luck with our wits and our hands. Now, you two." He pointed at the Bagshaws and shuffled toward the door. "You boys find me a Big Store. You find it fast."

"But . . ." Angus started.

Eddie glared. "Go."

And with that, Angus and Hamish were up and out the door.

Eddie looked around at the rest of them. "Why are you sitting here? We have work to do."

10 DAYS UNTIL
THE SALE

RURAL
CANADIAN COAST

CHAPTER 35

"Well, what do you think?" Angus squinted through the bright sun, staring up at the big abandoned building behind him. There were boards on the windows, a rough patch on the roof. Even in spring, the wind felt straight from the North Pole, and Kat shivered on the high bluff with the view of the icy Atlantic waters.

"*This* is the place?" Gabrielle asked. "We're supposed to believe a member of the Hale family has spent the last fifty years living . . . here?" She followed Kat through the front doors, past crumbling stairs and dirty windows, and didn't try to hide her disgust. Birds nested in the rafters. A squirrel ran across the floor.

"Is it cheap?" Kat asked.

"It's free." Angus gave a self-satisfied grin.

"Then it's perfect," Kat told him, and walked on.

"Hey, Kat!" Hamish yelled from the second story. "Don't worry about the lights. Dad had a . . . uh . . . *supply* of generators. We'll have the whole place lit up by tonight." He was running down the stairs, but then he hit a loose step, stumbled, and fell the rest of the way.

"We'll fix that," Angus told Kat.

"Good idea," Gabrielle said.

Kat walked on through the empty foyer. "What was this place again?"

"I don't know exactly." Angus shrugged. "The really old house of a really old rich dude, I guess. Felix found it. He ran the Monte Cristo here once. No one comes this far up the coast this early in the year, so we've got twenty square miles to ourselves."

"Good." Kat nodded her approval and headed down the hall, past someone carrying a massive stack of board games. "Is that Guido Romero?" Kat asked.

Angus shook his head. "Guido's having a little Interpol situation, so we got Antonio."

"Hey, Antonio!" Kat yelled, and she and Gabrielle and Angus walked on, past Uncle Ezra and Uncle Felix, who were engaged in a serious argument regarding a pair of fuzzy slippers.

"Do I want to know what that's about?" she whispered.

"No," Angus said, then led them into a room equipped with an upright piano, three Ping-Pong tables, and a massive aquarium. Angus took them through a library, which had been recently outfitted with every textbook Uncle Marco had stolen from the Cornell Medical School in 1983. There was a commercial-grade kitchen being cleaned by the Bagshaws' cousin Buster, a dining room being transformed into a parlor by the two DiMarcos who weren't currently in jail, and two Hungarian sisters who owed Uncle Eddie a very large favor were arguing over the best way to apply bars to the exterior windows.

"What's upstairs?" Gabrielle asked.

"Bedrooms," Angus said. "We'll try to keep them off-limits, but we'll have one ready to go if we need it."

"Good," Kat said.

Everywhere they walked, Kat smelled fresh paint and new two-by-fours. There was the constant humming of drills and banging of hammers, and Kat imagined she was backstage on Broadway, but judging by the butterflies in her stomach, she wasn't ready for the curtain to go up.

"Can we do something about the smell?" Gabrielle asked.

"We're running fans twenty-four hours a day, and in the morning we'll hit the whole place with that." Angus pointed to a pile of cleaning supplies in the corner. "We'll have it lemon-fresh by showtime, don't you worry."

"If they ask for paperwork?" Kat asked.

"Uncle Charlie is forging it personally," Angus said. "Should have it here by tonight. It's a shame we couldn't get him to bring it himself. We could have used the help."

"He's Uncle Eddie's identical twin, not his clone," Kat reminded him. "The paperwork will be enough. I hope."

They were almost back to the front door, and Kat was almost satisfied, when Hamish yelled, "Fire in the hole!" from somewhere on the second floor. Lights flashed. The roof shook. A fairly large bird's nest dislodged from the rafters and hit Gabrielle on the head.

"That's it," Gabrielle said. "I'm out of here."

"There may be a few kinks still," Angus admitted.

"Will you be ready?" Kat asked.

"Not a problem, Kitty," Angus said with a defiant nod.

"Angus . . ." Kat said, the word a warning.

For the first time since Kat had known him, Angus grew serious. "We won't let Hale down."

"Thanks."

"But, Kitty . . ." Angus ran a hand through his hair. Whatever he wanted to say was a struggle. "About ol' Hale . . . I was thinking that after what happened at the gala, maybe Hamish and I could keep an eye on him."

"Hale will be fine." Kat tried to wave the worry away.

"Will he?" Angus asked.

"Of course," she said, remembering that the biggest lies you tell are for yourself.

Kat wasn't surprised when she wasn't able to fall asleep. There was the stress, of course. Gabrielle's snoring never helped. But more than anything, Kat couldn't turn off her mind. There were too many things that could go wrong, and they kept playing one after another on a perpetual loop through her mind, so finally she gave up and went downstairs.

The thick railing was smooth beneath her hands, the rugs lush and soft beneath her bare feet. And Kat was content to creep through the big old house, just another ghost, right up until the point when she realized she wasn't alone.

"Some tea, miss?" Marcus said as soon as Kat stepped into the kitchen.

"Marcus, I didn't know you were here."

"Your uncle and I had a . . . cram session." He struggled over the slang, but didn't let it stop him. "I will be accompanying him in the morning. It is a very big day." He reached for the kettle and brought two cups to the table. "Cream or sugar?"

"You don't have to wait on me, Marcus," she told him. "Technically, this time, you're the client."

He smiled but didn't agree. "If you'll forgive me, miss, it is either work or worry. Work feels far more natural."

Kat found her favorite chair. "I know the feeling."

Marcus busied himself with the kettle and the cups. His hands shook a little in a way Kat had never seen before. He didn't face her when he asked, "Can he do this?"

"Uncle Eddie once pulled the Anastasia on a duke in Edinburgh. Trust me. If anyone can—"

Marcus shook his head. "Not your uncle."

Kat read his eyes, the set of his jaw, and she knew that Marcus's worries went far beyond his sister. She thought about the teenager who had gotten drunk and risked everything at the gala, the angry kid who had stormed into Garrett's office without a plan. She'd tried to tell herself that Hale was fine— he was good. But then there were the flashes of sorrow and rage, and Kat knew that he wasn't okay. He was just trying to con himself into thinking that he was.

"I've never seen Hale like this."

"If I may, miss . . ." Marcus gestured to the seat beside her.

"Please, Marcus. Sit. Talk to me."

He took the seat, but never really rested there. His back stayed straight. His hands stayed folded. Marcus was a man clinging to honor and responsibility, to family pride and the satisfaction of doing something very few people in the world still did well.

Kat totally knew the feeling.

251

"Has Mr. Hale ever told you how I came to be in his employ?"

"Yes." Kat laughed a little. "About a hundred times. I'm still waiting for the truth, though."

"I was the personal valet to Mr. Hale the Second. Marianne, of course, was a ladies' maid for Mrs. Hale. The two of us had been in those roles for as long as we could remember. I didn't know any other life."

"What happened?"

"When young Mr. Hale was six years old, his parents decided to sail around the world. Two days after they left, the nanny resigned and the cook quit. His parents knew this, of course, and yet they stayed away for six months and they left that child alone with a gardener."

He drew a deep breath, then talked on. "When his grandmother heard, she sent me to the country house to find him, and then she asked if I would consider caring for the boy myself. And that was where I stayed until the day you came for him."

"Technically, I didn't come for *him*," Kat said. "He's just what I left with."

"And I, for one, believe you got the better of that trade."

He stood and pushed in his chair.

"Marcus," Kat said, stopping him at the door. "If we fail—"

"I don't care if we lose the company, miss. But I would care a great deal if we lost the boy."

Kat nodded and let him go. There was nothing else to say.

9 DAYS UNTIL
THE SALE

~~REALLY OLD HOUSE OF A REALLY RICH DUDE~~

THE KELLER INSTITUTE FOR HIGHER MENTAL BEING, RURAL CANADIAN COAST

CHAPTER 36

By two o'clock the following afternoon, the cast members were in their places and the stage was finally set. Kat found herself on an overturned crate in a tiny upstairs room, sitting beside Simon and staring at the myriad of screens that covered the wall—the backstage of the con.

When the trio of dark SUVs pulled down the winding lane, Kat saw them from the window. Uniformed drivers stepped out and reached for the rear passenger doors, and Kat said, "Okay, Simon. The Big Store is open for business."

No sooner had she said the words than the front doors swung open and an old man yelled, "Come in!"

"Reginald!" Bobby yelled, chasing after Uncle Eddie. "Reginald, we talked about how the cold is bad for your leg." Bobby reached for Eddie's arm, but Eddie jerked away.

"Can't you see my family is here, doc?" Eddie glanced at Garrett, who stood wordless amid the throng. "All except that one. I don't have a clue about that one."

"I see that, Reg," Bobby said. "And I'm very much looking forward to meeting everyone . . . inside."

"I don't know why," Eddie said. "Bunch of worthless freeloaders. Never showed up before . . ." He spoke under his breath, the ramblings of a crazy man.

"Come on, Reg." Bobby gestured for the door. "Let's go in."

Slowly, the group made their way onto the rickety porch and through the big front doors. The stairs creaked. The floor moaned. And Kat's father just kept smiling, clipboard in hand.

"Now, Reginald, won't you introduce me to your friends?" Bobby asked.

"They're not my friends. They're my family."

Bobby gave a hearty laugh. "Oh, Reg, you are the life of the party."

A nurse walked by, and Eddie winked at her. The expression on his face was exactly like the one Reginald had worn in the family movies, and Kat must not have been the only one to see the similarities.

"Hello, Reginald," Hale's aunt said very, very slowly. "I'm *Elizabeth*. I am Hazel's *daughter*. That makes me your *niece*."

"I'm crazy, Liz," Reginald said. "Doesn't mean I'm stupid."

"No. No." Bobby gave a hearty laugh. "As you'll see, your uncle is in very good health for a man with his history."

"And who are you, exactly?" Hale's father puffed out his chest and looked skeptically at Bobby, who never wavered.

He just held out his hand and said, "Sorry about that. I'm

Dr. Nathaniel Jones. I'm your uncle's primary physician."

In the dim, quiet room upstairs, Kat whispered to Simon, "And the *real* Dr. Jones . . ."

"Has a Ph.D. from Harvard and an M.D. from Johns Hopkins, but recently decided to retire on a blissfully quiet beach in Belize."

"Perfect," Kat said, and kept her eyes glued to the screens.

Senior was walking through the foyer, staring at hastily patched walls and out-of-date fixtures. "What is this place?" he asked.

"This is your uncle's home." Bobby looked at W. W. Hale the Fourth as if he didn't know how a man could be so insensitive. "In fact, we're home for dozens of people like Reginald. People who have special needs. People for whom life in mainstream society might be stressful or even dangerous. For our residents, this isn't just a house—it's a haven."

"So it's an institution?" Senior said.

"Well . . ." Bobby hesitated, but then finally admitted, "that term is appropriate, but we do not prefer it."

"I would have preferred not to think my uncle was dead for five decades, but no one asked me."

"Would you like a tour?" Bobby asked, sweeping the clipboard out wide.

"I want some questions answered." Hale's uncle stepped forward. Kat watched the way his eyes cut around the room, taking everything in. "Such as, why hasn't our family physician ever heard of you or your facility?"

"Oh, well"—Bobby gave a throaty laugh—"we cater to patients who, shall we say, place a premium on discretion."

"What does that—" Senior started, but Hale cut him off.

"He means rich people." Hale looked at Bobby. "Isn't

that what you're saying? This is where the über-rich send their über-embarrassing, über-crazy branches of the family tree?"

Bobby lowered his gaze. "We've been entrusted with the care of some very special patients through the years. And we guard their privacy as ardently as we've guarded your uncle's."

Bobby gave a glance toward a series of photographs lining the walls. Bobby with a retired, reclusive senator. A member of the royal family playing dominoes with Uncle Eddie in the game room.

"Uncle Charlie forged those?" Kat asked.

"Uh-huh." Simon nodded, but Kat didn't feel any better.

"They're not buying it." She watched Garrett, who was still silent, almost bored, going through the paces of someone else's con. "He's going to squeal on us," Kat said.

"If he were going to squeal, he would have done it by now," Simon said. "He doesn't care about this. He just wants to sell his prototype and disappear. Now be quiet."

The tiny room that Simon had transformed into the communications base felt crowded, and Kat finally knew what was harder than running the long con: sitting on the sidelines and watching your long con go on without you.

"I'm hot. It's hot in here." She was all nerves and sweat, and spoke rapid-fire, fanning herself with an old magazine. "Is the computer room always so hot?"

"Sometimes the computer room is in an outhouse. In Mexico. In July. So, stop squirming."

Kat did as she was told. She didn't say a word when Simon picked up a microphone and said, "Uncle Felix, it's time."

Somewhere in the depths of the building, there was a cry, and then a very old, very naked man ran down the hall.

"Was it just me, or did we agree on underwear?" Kat asked.

"You know Felix," Simon said with a shrug. "He likes to improvise."

Downstairs, Felix was running circles around the Hale family, and Bobby was yelling, "Orderly!"

"On it!" Angus said, chasing after Felix with a robe.

"Sorry about that, folks," Bobby told his guests. "Never a dull moment around here, I can assure you. Now, where were we?"

"My brother and sister were trying to explain to you that this is quite a shock," Senior told Bobby.

"Oh, Felix? Don't worry about him. He's harmless. He just thinks the Nazis are tracking him through his clothes, or so he says. Really, he just likes being naked."

"Not . . . that." Hale's father gestured at the wrinkly blur that flashed across the end of the hall. "My uncle was dead, doctor. He was dead and gone, and now we are supposed to believe that he . . . isn't."

"I see how that could be quite a shock." Bobby nodded gravely. "Reginald has been with us for a long time, and—"

"How long?" Elizabeth wanted to know.

"Well, I'm afraid Reginald's medical records are private."

"I'm the man's next of kin—if he is who he says he is," Senior spat. "I demand to know."

"Reginald," Bobby asked, "what do you say to that?"

"Tell them what they want to know." Eddie eased closer to Hale's mother. "Your eyes look like K2 at sunrise."

"Oh, thank you," she said.

"Doctor," Senior said, trying to regain control.

"He's been here longer than I have. As you know, your

uncle was quite the explorer. When he was thirty-five, he was in a terrible plane crash. It shattered his leg and left him near death for many months."

"That's why he has that limp?" Senior asked.

Bobby nodded. "It is. The crash was in a very rural area. Local doctors did their best, but the leg never properly healed, and . . ." Bobby trailed off, looked at the floor. His voice softened. "And, in many ways, your uncle never truly recovered."

"The ladies love a limp," Eddie said with a wink.

"Yes they do, Reg. Yes they do." Bobby patted Eddie on the back. "We're very fond of your uncle, Mr. Hale. He's been here for a very long time, but don't make the mistake of thinking that he has been among strangers. Sometimes, people make their own family."

Kat didn't want to read too much into things, but she couldn't help thinking that her father was speaking about *her* Hale. Her family.

"Do you know, doctor . . ." Hale's father paused and then began again. "Do you know who this man is? Who he *claims* he is? And what those claims would mean?"

"Oh." Bobby laughed. "Reg has claimed to be a lot of people through the years. Haven't you, Reg? Let's see . . . sometimes he says he's descended from a duke. Then he'll tell anyone who will listen that he was the first American to scale K2. Why, just last week he told me he discovered a tribe in the Amazon—"

"That's true," Hale said, whispering. "All those things are true."

"You don't say?" Bobby asked, then looked at Eddie like he was seeing the man for the very first time.

260

"A name!" Senior spat. "Did you know his name?"

"Of course. He said his name was Reginald Hale."

"And you didn't think it was odd that Reginald Hale is supposed to be dead?" Hale's aunt asked.

Bobby tilted his head. "To tell you the truth, I was under the impression that the family knew Reginald was here."

"Why would you say that?" Senior asked.

"Why . . ." Bobby's eyes went wide in disbelief. In the dark, quiet room, Kat felt herself hold her breath. "Because of the checks, of course."

They'd reached a set of double doors, and Bobby pointed to the gold plaque beside them, stating that they were about to enter the Hazel Hale Recreation Room.

The Hale family stood speechless.

"I was very sorry to hear of her passing," Bobby told the family.

"Why . . ." Senior stumbled over the thought. "Why are you contacting us now? My uncle has been gone for half a century. Why didn't he stay gone?"

Bobby removed his glasses, and when he spoke, he couldn't hide the guilt in his voice. "I guess that's because the checks . . . stopped."

"If he is who he says he is, he'll have to prove it," Senior told them.

Bobby looked at Eddie. "I'm sure Reginald wouldn't mind. Would you, Reg?"

"I climbed K2," Eddie said in response.

"So he has no family?" Hale's uncle asked.

Bobby looked confused. "I thought you were his family."

"He means heirs," Hale said. "What about it, Reg? When you die, who's going to get your half?"

"Scooter!" Elizabeth said, feigning offense. "But I wonder, Uncle Reg, *do* you have any children?"

Eddie took her in. "Maybe I'll adopt you."

"If you'd like us to perform a DNA test, I can recommend a very good facility not too far—" Bobby said, but Hale's father's laugh cut him off.

"A billion-dollar corporation is on the line," Senior said. "We'll find our own lab, thank you very much." Then he spoke to the lawyer. "You'll take care of that, won't you, Garrett?"

Until then, the trustee had stayed at the back of the group, glancing at his watch, staring at the walls. Mentally, the man was already far away, on an island with his stolen fortune. Reginald didn't matter to his plan. This was nothing more than a delay. An annoyance. And whatever became of the Hales, both long-lost and not, would be none of his concern in a matter of days.

If Kat hadn't hated him so much, she might have warned him he was making a classic newbie mistake.

"What's that?" Garrett asked.

"The DNA test," Senior said again. "You *will* handle that, won't you?"

"Oh," Garrett said. "Of course. Right away."

Then he walked purposefully down the hall, past a very naked Felix running from a very frustrated Hamish, and into the cold.

The rest of the Hale family delegation wasn't far behind, but at the doors, Hale stopped briefly. Simon had placed cameras at each entrance, standard for any facility of the kind. And Hale looked squarely into one, mouthed the words *Bye, Kat* to the girl he knew was watching.

And then he was out the door. And then he was gone.

"What do you think, Kat?" Simon asked, turning to her.

"I think we're ready for phase two."

"It would have been easier just to let the Bagshaws kidnap Garrett," Simon said.

Kat sat there silently, not wanting to admit he was right.

8 DAYS UNTIL THE SALE

NEW JERSEY, USA

CHAPTER 37

When Kat walked into the lab, it was decidedly different from the first time she'd seen it. Before, there had been dust and grime, a smell of disuse and old chemicals, and it had felt a little like walking into a tomb. But now, everything was alive. Music boomed from the back room (classic jazz); spotlights cut through the dark. There were at least a dozen whiteboards lining the walls, each covered with the same kinds of formulas and checklists she'd seen in Silas's original lab.

Kat felt fascinated and out of her depth, but that was nothing compared to the magnetic pull of the small device that sat on a tray in the center of the room, bright lights shining down upon it.

"Hello, Miss Bishop."

Kat pulled away from the prototype as if Silas's voice were a warning, and she'd been caught.

"You can touch it," he told her. "It won't bite."

Kat smiled, embarrassed. "Sorry. I just . . . I don't understand any of this."

"That's okay," Silas told her. "I don't understand what you do. From where I'm standing, that makes us even."

"So how's it going?" She was almost afraid to ask, but she had to know.

"Fine." Silas took a seat on a stool and eyed his design. "I think. Maybe."

Kat totally knew the feeling.

"How was your Big Score?" Silas asked.

"Our what?" Kat asked, then had to laugh. "Oh, the Big *Store*? It went as well as could be expected. It bought us a little more time, at least."

A wide smile spread across the old man's face. If Kat didn't know better, she would have sworn he was having the time of his life.

"I'm glad to have my assistant back." Silas pointed to Simon, who was dragging computers and cables into the back room.

"I thought you had help?" Kat asked.

Just then, Simon's father came into the lab and yelled, "Hey, Kat!"

"Hi, Uncle Henry. Thanks for coming."

"No problem," Henry said, then returned to work.

"The father is good," Silas said. "But the son is . . . special."

Kat stole a glance at Simon, who was sorting through the cables and the cords, lost in another world. "Yeah. He is. So,

Silas, really . . ." Kat touched his hand. She searched his eyes. "How is it going?"

"We're close," he said, then took off his glasses and looked down at the device on the table. "Just not quite close enough."

"How long do you need?"

He rubbed his eyes. "I wish I could say."

"That's okay, Silas. Just do your best. We're working on Plan B."

"Kat!" Simon yelled from the back room. "I think you need to hear this."

"What is it?" Kat asked as soon as she reached the office that Simon called his own.

His eyes were wide and his breath was labored as he told her, "Our guy has company." He pulled the cord that connected his headphones to his computer, and instantly, voices came through the laptop speakers, filling the room.

"What are you doing in my office?"

Kat watched Garrett through the cameras that she and Hale had installed on their visit to the thirty-seventh floor. The lawyer was up and moving around his desk. For a moment he blocked the camera, but the voice that came through the microphone was one Kat had definitely heard before.

"I thought perhaps it was time I paid you a little visit."

That voice. That accent.

"Ms. . . ."

"Montenegro," the woman supplied her name, assuming, Kat supposed, that Garrett would have forgotten it. "You haven't called me, Mr. Garrett." She pouted. "If I were a different sort of woman my feelings would be hurt."

"Really, Ms. Montenegro, this is not the time or the place."

She looked around. "It seems the perfect time and a . . . somewhat acceptable place." She bent forward in a way that afforded the man a glimpse of cleavage. "Don't you want to hear my offer?"

"I have a buyer." Garrett rubbed his hands together nervously and looked toward the door.

"A buyer who can have the money in your account by the end of the day? Where do you want it? Switzerland? Cayman Islands?"

"No. No." Garrett tried to walk away, but the woman deftly cut him off.

"The only thing I don't understand is why you haven't sold it yet. Are you getting soft, Garrett? Or . . . no. Wait. Don't tell me the Chinese are holding off until the Hale model proves faulty."

Kat could tell by the look on Garrett's face that she was right. The woman must have seen it too, because she talked on.

"My employer can afford to be far more . . . flexible. We don't care if the Hales claim copyright infringement. What's a little piracy between enemies?"

She rose and strolled around the small office, eyed the paperwork piled on the desk.

"But if you want to stay here, keep on keeping up appearances, being the good little worker . . ." The words struck a nerve, and she saw it. "Oh, you must hate them so."

"I appreciate your coming, Ms. Montenegro. But I'm afraid I already have a buyer." He stood up straighter, as if forcing himself to literally be strong. "Now, I think you'd better leave."

Long after the door was closed and the screen was vacant, Kat could still hear herself breathing.

"Kat . . ." Simon said her name carefully, cautiously. It sounded like he was afraid she was sleepwalking and didn't know how to wake her. "What do we do now?"

"What else can we do? We get ready to rob the most secure bank in the world."

CHAPTER 38

The Superior Bank of Manhattan was not the largest bank in the city. It wasn't the most famous. What the Superior Bank of Manhattan was was *infamous*, so Kat couldn't quite steady her nerves as she walked through the front doors, even with her father by her side.

"So this is what you do now?" Bobby asked, but Kat just made a mental note of the position of the cameras.

"I'm pretty sure it's what I've *always* done."

"Yeah, but before you had parental supervision." Kat gave her father a questioning look, so he shrugged. "Parental proximity," he conceded. "Anyway, this is nice." He slipped an arm around her shoulders. "Almost like old times." He gave a squeeze, and Kat realized how much she'd missed him.

She sank into the hug, rested her head against his shoulder, and said, "Dad . . ."

"What is it, sweetie?"

Kat felt especially young that day, walking through the massive lobby, her father at her side. But she couldn't bring herself to say so, so she glanced at the security cameras and asked her father, "Are those the nine-sixties?"

"You know perfectly well they are," he told her. "Now, what is it?"

She didn't have a lie that would work, so she settled on the truth. "This job is different."

"I know."

"I don't think we can do it. And I'm not sure we should."

Kat felt the lobby around her beating like a pulse. Employees hustled from desk to desk. People stood in line at the teller windows. A few VIPs were escorted to and from private offices in the back. And, through it all, armed guards stood at every entrance.

Hale Industries sat on the bank's east side, a police station on the west, and beneath it all, a custom-designed bank vault that had never before been cracked. Inside that, there were one thousand safety deposit boxes, any one of which could have held the prototype and plans.

Simon was the genius, but even Kat knew enough not to like that math.

"So what are you thinking, Kat?"

"I'm thinking it's impossible."

"Now, that's not the daughter I raised. Nothing is impossible."

"No." Kat shook her head. "No. It is."

"What about the Fiddler on the Roof?" her father asked. "We could always—"

"What, Dad? What could we possibly do that's going to make this right?" She looked slowly around the building, her mind racing with the things she didn't have to say.

Uncle Felix was reaching out to a source he had in the bank fraud division of the FBI, and the Bagshaws were convinced there was a way to tunnel in from an old subway station that hadn't been used since World War II, but in her heart, Kat knew it was all useless.

"He's a step ahead of us," Kat told him. She could feel it in her bones, and she hated it. "He has been from the beginning, and now . . ."

"You know what you do when something's in your way?" Bobby asked, testing her.

"Go around," Kat said with a roll of her eyes.

"Exactly." Bobby flashed a wide, bright grin.

He made it sound so easy. He always did. But it wasn't easy, and Kat knew it. "It's just . . ."

"What?" Bobby asked with a jerk of his head, as if trying to pull the question out.

"What if I can't do it this time?" Kat admitted.

"The whole family's working on it, kiddo. You're not in this one alone."

"What if it's too late? I mean, the wrong plans are on file at the patent office. Even if we get the prototype, Hale Industries can't use it without—"

"One job at a time, kiddo. One job at a time."

Her father was right, and Kat knew it. But she was also a little mad that he'd broken off a perfectly good pity party with logic. Kat didn't want a way to rob the Superior Bank of

Manhattan. She wanted a way for it to be over. All of it. She just didn't have a clue what that way might be.

Then she heard her name echo through the lobby.

"Kat!" Natalie called. "Oh my gosh. Fancy seeing you here."

"Yeah," Kat said, her mind whirling. "Fancy that. What are you doing here?"

"Funny." Nat gave her a smile. "I was about to ask you the same thing." Then she shifted her attention onto Bobby. "Who's your friend?"

"Robert Bishop." Bobby extended his hand. "I'm Kat's father."

"Natalie Garrett," Natalie told him, then gave the slight swoon that Kat had become accustomed to women giving in her father's presence. Natalie eyed his dark suit and power tie and said, "What kind of business are you in, Mr. Bishop? If you don't mind my asking."

"Acquisitions," Bobby said.

"How fascinating," Natalie said with a bat of her eyes.

"It has its moments," Bobby said. "Okay, girls, I'll leave the two of you alone."

"You're leaving?" Kat asked.

"Yeah, sweetheart. I really should get back to work."

"But . . ."

"I'm going to go find a way around," he told her, then planted a kiss on her cheek. "Love you," he said and walked toward the doors without a single glance back.

"So, your dad's hot."

"Thanks. He was that way when I met him, so I can't really take credit."

"That's too bad." Natalie popped a piece of chewing gum

275

into her mouth, offered the pack to Kat, and said, "So is he the one who stuck you in Knightsbury?"

Over Natalie's shoulder, the service entrance opened and two guards came out, changing shifts. Kat noted the time: four-fifteen.

"Hello," Natalie said, annoyed. "Earth to Kat."

"Colgan," Kat said, distracted. "First, I went to Colgan."

"So you met Scooter there?"

"Uh . . . no," Kat said. "He was already gone before I showed up. And got kicked out."

Natalie laughed. "No! Really? *You* got kicked out of Colgan?"

"Sure did."

"Cool," Natalie said, finally impressed. She blew a big bubble then popped it with her finger. "Oh, I'm sorry. Was there something you needed to do?"

"No. I just came in for some cash," Kat said, pointing at the ATM.

"Oh. Cool."

Walking with Natalie, out the front doors of the bank and onto the busy sidewalk, Kat felt especially alone.

"Well, I guess I'll see you around, Kat."

"Yeah, Nat," Kat told her. "See you around."

Hale said they weren't supposed to use her—that she had no place in what they had to do. And maybe he was right. Maybe it was a coincidence, seeing her in the very place Garrett had stashed the prototype—the bank that Kat and her crew needed to rob. But Kat had learned at a very young age not to believe in coincidences. She watched Nat walk away, gave a little wave when the girl glanced back.

She was still staring after her when a dark shadow fell over Kat's shoulder, and she felt Hamish and Angus beside her.

"Don't let her out of your sight," she told them.

"Yes, ma'am," they said, and together they started down the sidewalk, dissolving into the crowds.

CHAPTER 39

For the rest of the day, Kat couldn't stop pacing. She bit her nails and twisted her hair, anything to keep moving, thinking, breathing in and out. Anything to fight the feeling that something was wrong.

"Kat, you're going to wear a hole in the floor," Simon told her. "And I really like this lab."

Silas was still at work on the prototype, but Simon's office had morphed into a not-exactly-to-scale replica of the bank, and Kat totally didn't like what she saw. Lasers and cameras and guards, a vault door that would require a nuclear bomb to blast through, and a maze of safety deposit boxes in a deep, dark room, any one of which could have been the box they needed.

"Don't worry, Kat." Simon must have read her mind, because he placed a hand awkwardly on her back and patted. "It'll work out."

But Kat didn't feel so sure.

Something felt off about the job or the day or maybe both. She couldn't quite name it, and the not-knowing was the worst feeling of all.

"How was the scouting trip?" Simon asked.

"Weird," Kat said.

"Was it the motion detectors? Because I think I have a way around—"

"Natalie." The word was a whisper, and yet it made Simon stop cold.

"What about her?"

"She was there."

"Why?" Simon asked.

Kat bit her nails. "That's what I really want to know. The Bagshaws are tailing her now. There's just something about that girl I don't trust. Gab would say I'm acting jealous, but—"

"Are you?" Simon asked.

Kat shrugged. "Maybe. But I still don't like it. She's always around and a little too accommodating. She reminds me of . . . me."

"Then clearly she can't be trusted."

"Exactly!"

"Kat!" Angus's voice boomed through the lab. "Simon, I'm home."

"I thought you said they were tailing Natalie?" Simon asked.

"I thought they were."

A moment later, Angus came pushing through the office door.

"Never to worry, love," he said before Kat could scold him for abandoning his post. "She's just popped into Daddy's office. Hamish is waiting for her outside, but I thought I'd—"

"Simon, call up the feed to Garrett's office."

"He's not doing anything interesting. He never does anything interesting. Except for that one meeting, the office bug hasn't given us—"

"Just call it up. I want to see what the two of them are talking about."

Simon didn't have to be asked again. Soon, a familiar image filled the screen, but something about it was off.

"Where's Natalie?" Kat asked.

"I dunno," Angus said. "Maybe she's already gone."

Kat reached for a phone and dialed. "Hey, Hamish, what's Natalie's location?"

"She's in the Hale Building," Hamish's scratchy voice answered through the speakerphone. "Probably talking to her dad."

"No." Kat kept her eyes glued to the screen, at where Nat's father sat stoically at his desk, talking to no one. "She's not."

"Maybe she went to see someone else? It is a big building," Simon guessed, but another thought had occurred to Kat. She saw the way Garrett sat at his desk—so still. No sudden movements.

"The bug Gabrielle put on his watch at the gala. Is that still active?"

"I don't know," Simon said. "Probably."

"Turn it on. Now."

As soon as Simon punched the keys, the image on the screen stayed the same, but the voices were new.

"Hello, Father. Nice of you to see me. It's not so nice to keep me waiting."

"What do you want, Natalie?"

"We have trouble."

"I'm busy."

"Well, I've been busy too. Trying to lose the doofus Kat Bishop had following me, for starters."

"Clearly that girl is talking about Hamish," Angus said, but Kat didn't have time for bruised egos. She was too busy studying the picture that absolutely did not match the sound.

"And the highlight of my afternoon was a trip to the bank." Natalie talked on, but she was still nowhere to be seen. It was almost like the video they were watching had been faked. Staged.

"They looped our feed." Kat's voice was full of disbelief. "We've been looped."

It was exactly what Kat would have done—what she *had* done on a number of occasions—and she felt the sting that comes from knowing that turnabout is absolutely not fair play.

"They must have found the cameras." Simon looked like someone had just killed his puppy, but Kat closed her eyes, absorbed by every word.

"What are you talking about?" Garrett asked his daughter.

"I just met Bobby Bishop. He's more handsome than he looks in his mug shot. Charming, too."

"Natalie, I don't have time for this," Garrett said, but there was a slamming sound, like a hand on the desk.

"They're going to rob the bank." Natalie enunciated each

word so clearly there could be no mistaking what she'd said.

"Don't be silly. We chose that bank because it has never been robbed," her father said.

"No. *I* chose that bank. And I was the one watching it this afternoon. And I am telling you that Scooter and his merry band of thieves are casing the joint. My guess is we have a day or two at the most."

"That's ridiculous. They're kids."

"News flash, Dad. *I'm* a kid! Do not underestimate them." Her voice broke, and Kat thought she could just as easily have been saying *Do not underestimate me.*

"If you think Scooter and his friends are just kids, Dad, you're delusional. Besides, the girl's father isn't a kid. Neither is her uncle. I'm telling you, we've got to move up the meeting with the buyer."

"We don't *have* to do anything," Garrett shot back.

"Listen to me."

"No, you listen! You're not in charge here. I am. I'm the one who's taking all the risks. I'm the one who changed the old woman's will. The family would still be huddled around Hazel's bedside if it weren't for me, so don't get high and mighty," he huffed.

"What do you mean?"

"I'm the one who forged the Do Not Resuscitate order," he said. "So don't act all innocent. This was your idea, as you love to point out."

"Are we recording this?" Kat asked.

"Not that feed," Simon said, eyes wide, and Kat felt her heart plummet.

"I never said anything about a DNR." Natalie's voice

cracked. "I never said . . . I never wanted . . . Hazel was good to me."

"Hazel was a Hale. You don't know them like I do." Kat could hear him shoving papers around, tidying up for the night. "She was dying, Natalie. I just made sure it happened before she could fire me and ruin everything."

"You killed her."

"I did her a favor!"

It was like it wasn't really happening—like Kat was listening to an old-time radio show about deceit and betrayal, and she sat waiting for the scene to end.

"Don't worry, Natalie. I'll leave an anonymous tip with the FBI. No one is going to rob that bank this week." The door opened. "Are you coming?" he asked as if they had never fought at all.

The silence that came next was the longest Kat had ever heard. No one moved. No one breathed. No one did a thing until a voice came from the back of the room, asking, "That was Natalie?"

Kat didn't know when Hale had come in or how much he'd heard, but the look in his eyes said that it was enough.

"It was Natalie's idea?" he asked, then swallowed hard. "And Hazel . . . she didn't have a DNR?" He nodded slowly, as if taking it all in. "That makes sense. She would have wanted to fight. She would have hung on for as long as she could. Yeah," he said, sounding resolved. "That makes sense."

"Hale . . ." Kat was up and walking toward him.

"You know what, Kat, I don't really feel like working today." He was moving, backing away. "I'll talk to you later."

"Hale!" Kat yelled, but he was already through the lab and out the door.

She ran after him, but by the time she reached the parking lot, there was nothing left but tire tracks and a cloud of dust.

CHAPTER 40

Kat had run away once. And even though she could have gone anywhere—done anything—she had chosen the Colgan School, with its manicured lawns and ivy-covered towers. She had run to Hale's world. And Hale had run to hers. Perhaps they were destined to meet somewhere, at some time along the way. And maybe they were both destined to someday return to the worlds that had made them.

She would have traded everything she knew for one glimpse at where he might have run to on that night, but it wasn't possible, so she didn't try. All she could do was send the rest of her crew out looking, dispersing into the city, trying to chase the boy that, if Kat knew him at all, wouldn't be caught until he was good and ready.

So Kat walked through the streets of Brooklyn alone, all

the way to a familiar stoop and a wooden door, and the smells of the Old Country drifting from the kitchen.

But something else, too. Voices. Deeper, darker, and older than the ones she had grown accustomed to hearing.

"Casper the Friendly Ghost?" somebody said as Kat crept slowly closer.

"Doesn't get us past the cameras," Uncle Sal said. "What about the Rumpelstiltskin?"

"No good." Uncle Felix threw his hands in the air. "My hypnotist moved to Phoenix. Emphysema."

They all shook their heads and muttered, "Poor Madame Zelda."

"Have a seat, sweetie." Uncle Ezra seemed to be the only one who noticed Kat's presence. He pulled out a chair and gestured for her to take it. "We're trying to solve your problem. Any word on the kid?"

Kat rested her hands on the table, felt the smooth wood beneath her palms. "Angus and Hamish and Gabrielle are out looking for him. I thought he might come here, so . . ."

"He'll be okay, sweetheart." Ezra patted her hand. "Where's your pop?"

"Gone," Kat said.

"Already?" Felix seemed shocked, but then shrugged as if to say that he wasn't one to judge.

"They're on to us," Kat said. She felt embarrassed, ashamed. "We're made. They've known what Hale's been up to for months. Years, maybe. And now they know we're casing the bank, so . . . we can't hit the bank."

"We heard already," Uncle Felix said, with a shake of his head. "Tough break, sweetheart, but don't worry. We're on it."

"They're going to tip the FBI to watch the bank. *We*

can't hit the bank." Kat was repeating herself but she didn't know how to stop. She couldn't have run this con if her life depended on it. And in a way, Kat knew, it did.

Uncle Eddie stood by his stove. He said nothing and heard everything, and not for the first time in Kat's life, she would have given anything to know what he was thinking. But he just ladled soup into a bowl and pulled off a chunk of fresh bread and placed the meal before her.

She felt six years old again, safe and warm, sitting at the grown-ups' table with the men who had raised her. Family. Kat was among her family, and Hale was out in the cold. When Felix reached to butter her bread, Kat felt her eyes go moist, and she couldn't take it anymore. She pushed out of her chair and stepped toward the door.

"Hey, kiddo," Uncle Sal said. "Where ya going?"

Kat had to stop and look at them all. They were older, wiser. Crankier. At some point in the past dozen or so years, the hairlines had become a little thinner and the middles a little thicker. Her whole life, the men at that table had been teaching, guiding, protecting her at every step along the way. They were there to do it again, no matter what the consequences. It was time, Kat felt, to return the favor.

"I'm going to end it."

No one asked what she was doing. Not a soul told her not to go. It was her job, her con, her call. So the next step, they all knew, was hers.

"Katarina." Uncle Eddie's voice stopped her at the door. "I'll be here when you get back."

CHAPTER 41

When Kat walked out of the subway station, it was just starting to rain. The cold wind stung her skin. Fat drops clung to her lashes, water running down her cheeks with every blink until she had no idea whether or not she might be crying. She walked on, instinct and intuition guiding her steps until she found the building and went inside, as if there were never any doubt that she belonged.

The lock was easy enough to handle. The security code she already knew. So the hard part, as always, was the waiting. She sat silently in the dark, the Manhattan shadows looming all around her. And when the door began to open, she wasn't even a little bit afraid. After all, she was perfectly accustomed to being inside a man's world and in way over her head.

Kat flipped on the light and watched the man throw his

hands up to shield his eyes as she said, "Did I scare you? Oh, I hope I didn't scare you. . . ."

Garrett didn't say anything, but the rise and fall of his chest was more than answer enough.

"Mr. Garrett!" A burly man appeared in the doorway behind him, and in a flash was moving in Kat's direction. "Hands up," he told her.

"Easy, big guy," Kat said. "Mr. Garrett and I are old friends, isn't that right?"

"Do you know her?" the goon asked, and Kat watched Garrett consider the question. Did he know her? Did anyone, really?

Then he waved the goon away and said, "She's okay. I think. But you might want to . . . check her or something."

"Hands up," the goon told her again.

"Really, you're going to need to buy me dinner first," Kat said, but she went ahead and raised her hands and let the goon pat her down.

"She's clean," the man told his boss, then stepped back and stood at attention.

Garrett nodded, comfortable with the power that comes from hired muscle and an underage target. Kat knew just how powerless she was supposed to be in that moment. She felt it in every one of her underaged, undersized bones. But she couldn't bring herself to tremble. She knew too well what she had to do.

"You hired a bodyguard, Mr. Garrett." She threw her hands to her chest and sounded especially girlie when she told him, "All for little ol' me. I'm flattered."

"Come, Kat. Surely you know that a man in my position requires some additional . . . insurance," he said, then studied her. "Why are you smiling?"

"No reason." Kat shrugged. "Your type of bad never really understands how to protect yourself against my type of bad. That's all."

"You are a talented girl," he said.

"You're not the first man to tell me that." She looked the attorney up and down. "The other guy was scarier. But at least he didn't pretend he wasn't a killer."

"I don't know what you're talking about."

"Oh, I think you do. You didn't pull a trigger, but Hazel is dead because of you, and I know it. And I'm not the only one."

"So . . ." Garrett walked into the small kitchen, opened a bottle, and poured himself a drink. "You're here to . . . what? Warn me? Make a deal? Ask for a cut?"

"No, thank you."

"I have no problem with you or your family, Miss Bishop. This was never about *your* family."

"Hale is my family."

Garrett gave a sickly sweet smile and put the cap back on the bottle. "That's nice. But as I was saying, it's not about you. Your father and your uncle and . . . whoever those other people are . . . they aren't a part of this. I have nothing against you and yours. The good people at Interpol, however—I can't speak for them."

He took an intimidating step closer to Kat, looming over her as he said, "But if you continue to stand between me and my affairs, I will make a phone call, and you won't like the results."

He shifted, waiting for the threat to land, and when it didn't, he narrowed his eyes and snapped, "What?"

"You're missing the point," Kat told him. "You know who I am. Good job, by the way. But I also know who you are. *And I know what you did.*"

"Are you going to say that makes us even?"

Kat glared. *"Not even close."*

She couldn't stand the sight of him, so she turned to the windows. "As we speak, copies of Hazel Hale's DNR are circulating to the best handwriting experts in the world—one of whom happens to be my uncle Charlie. That part is already in motion—there's nothing you can do about it now." She looked back at him, leveled him with her stare. "There are just two options for what happens next."

"And they are . . ." he asked, humoring her.

"Maybe those reports make their way to any number of people who can make your life difficult."

"I will soon be a very wealthy man. I don't care about difficult."

"You will if it means you can't sell the prototype. You see, Mr. Garrett, I can call the authorities, too."

"You have no proof."

"Oh, Garrett"—Kat made a *tsk tsk tsk* sound—"I can *make* proof. Or I can steal it. In any case, you don't want me as an enemy."

"And the second option?"

"You give me ten million dollars and this all goes away."

He couldn't stop himself from chuckling. "Ten million? That's all? That won't support your boyfriend's lifestyle for a year."

"It's not for me, and it's not for Hale."

"Then who is it for?"

"Marianne." Kat laughed a little at his naiveté. They had come all this way and still he didn't see the truth. "It was always for Marianne."

"The maid?"

"The person you wrote out of the will. That was a stupid move, by the way. If you'd left her in, none of this would have happened."

"Oh, I know." He took a sip of his drink and rolled his eyes. "But Hazel wanted her to be the trustee, and I couldn't have that, could I? She always was annoyingly honest."

"Good people have a tendency to be that way. Makes me glad I don't know that many."

"Okay. The maid gets ten million. And that's it?" He looked at Kat as if she were some rare species of human being. "You're not going to try to save your boyfriend's family business?"

"No, Mr. Garrett." Kat slipped on her jacket and crossed the room. "I'm trying to save my boyfriend."

Walking to the door, Kat knew she should have felt at ease. It was over. Almost. But something tugged at her, a lingering doubt she couldn't silence, a steady whisper in her ear.

"Just one more thing." Kat suddenly stopped. "Hale never sees you—or your daughter—again."

A condescending smile spread across Garrett's face.

"Anything else?"

"Do we have a deal, Mr. Garrett?"

He nodded. "Deal."

"Tomorrow at noon. Grand Central Station. I'll expect you there in person."

"And have you show up with the authorities? I don't think so."

"Fine," Kat conceded. "We'll do it in . . . Niagara Falls. On the Canadian side. Far out of New York jurisdiction. How does that sound?"

"I didn't peg you for a tourist."

"Let's just say I'm a girl who appreciates a crowd. There's a scenic overlook a mile past the border. Bring ten million in untraceable bonds and don't be late. If you are, I will personally make sure every member of my family knows there's a price on your head. You'd be surprised how many of them are good at stealing people."

The man smiled and held out his hand. "It's a pleasure doing business with you."

"Forgive me if I can't say the same."

CHAPTER 42

It didn't matter how close Kat sat to the fire in Uncle Eddie's drawing room; she still couldn't get warm. She kept seeing Garrett's cold smile, his black eyes. And she kept wondering if Hale would ever forgive her, knowing he was the one person whom she could never, ever con into forgetting her mistakes.

"Out of the frying pan . . ." she said to herself, unable to shake the feeling that it was just a matter of time until she got burned.

"You didn't eat." Uncle Eddie's voice was gruff and sleepy as he came into the room. "Come, Katarina. I'll make you something."

"I'm not hungry," she told him, and the old man shrugged.

"That's a pity." He dropped into a chair not far away. "My hands." He looked down, held them against the light of the fire. "I don't know what to do with them. It would have been nice to have a task."

"Sorry. I wish I could be more help."

He gave a shrug as if to say he'd grown used to disappointment, then propped a foot up on the coffee table, which was covered with photos and albums, the prep materials that nobody really needed anymore.

"I wish I'd known her." Kat picked up the album that showed an image of Hale's grandmother on her wedding day, standing between Reginald and her new husband.

"Have the boys found him?" Eddie asked, and Kat shook her head. The old man drew a deep breath then leaned back in his chair. "Your young man will be fine, Katarina."

"I know," Kat said.

"All young men must find their way. Yours is just a little off course at the moment."

"He misses Hazel."

Eddie nodded slowly. "I'm sure he does."

And then Eddie struggled to his feet. Kat hated those moments—the seconds, really, where his hands would shake or his knees subtly refused to bear his weight. There was nothing as painful to Katarina Bishop as the gentle reminders that she was not the only member of her family who was growing older, that someday she too would be left with nothing but a book full of pictures and memories.

"If I lost you . . ." Kat's voice broke. She couldn't meet his eyes, so she stared down at the flames.

"You're not going to lose me, Katarina."

"Promise?"

Eddie gave her shoulder a squeeze. "Would I lie?"

She wanted to believe him, to know that it was true. But

there were some things even the great Uncle Eddie couldn't stop—and fate, as it turned out, was one of them.

"Go to sleep, Katarina. This thing we do tomorrow . . . it is not an easy thing."

"Is it the right thing?" she asked.

He nodded. "It is the *best* thing. And that is all any grifter can hope for."

She heard him shuffle down the hall. A moment later, a door opened and closed, and Kat was left alone with her thoughts and the fire and the spinning earth that was slowly making its way toward tomorrow.

DAY OF
THE DEAL

NIAGARA FALLS,
CANADA

CHAPTER 43

Anything that can go wrong . . . will. It was the law of the grift, the rule of the con. If the mark is told to come alone, he won't. If you're supposed to have three exit routes, you'll be lucky to get one. And never, ever believe a weatherman when he says it isn't going to rain.

So Kat was more than a little surprised to see the sun so bright and clear overhead as she stepped out onto the wide scenic area overlooking the falls. Mist clung to the air, and a rainbow formed over the waters below, and it was beautiful, there at the top of the world. She might have actually enjoyed it if her whole body hadn't been trembling.

"Deep breaths, Katarina," Uncle Eddie said. "It steadies the nerves."

As was her habit, she took her uncle's advice.

At least two dozen tourists were already there, posing for pictures with the falls at their back, plugging quarters into the big old-fashioned machines that could let a person see right down onto the rocky shores. Kat counted ten cars and one school bus, but none of them belonged to the man who had completely ruined her May.

"Maybe he's not coming," she said, jamming her gloved hands deeper into her pockets.

"He'll be here," Eddie said. He sounded so certain, so sure, so at home there at the end of a job.

"What if this is the wrong call?"

"It is the only call, Katarina." He gave her a long look that she'd never seen before. He sounded different, not like he was talking to his niece, but like he was talking to a peer. "This is how it ends."

"Thank you." Kat reached out and took his hands. "Thank for doing this. Thank you for always being there for me."

"That, Katarina, is my job." He looked out over the horizon. "And my pleasure."

She stood on her tiptoes and kissed his cheek.

"Kat?" Simon's voice was in her head.

"Blasted contraptions." Eddie flinched and poked a finger in his ear, but Kat stopped him before he could pull the earbud out.

"What is it, Simon?" Kat said.

"Our guy is heading your way."

She looked at Uncle Eddie. "It's showtime."

The two of them stepped away from the road and watched a black SUV pull into the overlook, its big tires crunching in the gravel. Kat stood waiting for her first sight of Garrett, but instead, the driver's-side door opened, and the goon from the night before stepped out.

"Hands up," the hired thug said, and Kat had to laugh a little. The thug, however, didn't see what was funny.

"Old man. Teenage girl." Kat pointed between her uncle and herself, but the goon didn't seem to know that, for all their skills, neither Eddie nor Kat were really known for their physical prowess, so he patted them down just the same.

"They're clean," he yelled, and only then did the back door open.

"Yay," Kat said when Garrett emerged. "You're here."

"You've got a smart mouth," he told her.

Eddie shrugged. "It runs in the family."

"Oh yes," Garrett said, stepping slowly around them. "Uncle Reginald. Or is it Edward? It's so good to see you again."

"Can we get this over with?" Kat asked.

Garrett held his hands out wide. "You're the boss."

"Did you bring it?" Kat asked.

"You'll get your money."

"It's not for me," Kat said again. "It's for—"

"The maid," Garrett cut her off. "I know. I know. You're . . . noble."

"Yeah. You should try it sometime," Kat said.

Garrett looked at the goon and commanded, "Give me the case."

The man walked to the SUV and pulled out a silver briefcase. He handed it to Garrett, who held it like it was precious, gripping it too tightly for Kat's liking.

"Are you going to hand that over nicely or do we need to have a talk about honor among thieves?" she asked, but before the man could answer, a car pulled into the overlook.

It was different from the minivans and tour buses. Black and sleek, and driven by a chauffer named Marcus.

"Oh, no," Kat said, but Hale was already out of the car and moving toward her.

"Kat?" His voice was too soft somehow. It scared her. "Kat, what is going on? What are you doing here . . . with *him?*"

"It's okay, Hale." Kat moved gingerly toward him. "Why don't you go wait in the car and I'll explain in a little—"

"What are you doing here?" He looked between Kat and Eddie and then finally to the man with the silver case.

"Hale, wait. It's not what it—"

"What? *Looks like? Sounds like?* What's in the case, Kat?"

"He's going to pay Marianne. We're going to be able to take care of her."

"So you're here to make a deal with the man who killed my grandmother? I'm so glad I didn't jump to any conclusions."

"Hale . . ." Kat lunged to block his way. "Hale, calm down."

"I'm not going to calm down!" he shouted, and it felt to Kat like the whole mountain trembled. She half feared an avalanche. Tourists stared. School groups snapped pictures. But she couldn't do a thing to stop him.

"You killed Hazel," Hale said. "You!"

Hale lunged toward Garrett. He might have reached him, too—might have killed him—had the goon not been there. He reached for Hale and held him back, squeezed his arms against his side. Garrett looked at the boy.

"You never learned your place, Scooter." He pulled back a fist.

"No!" Kat shouted, but Eddie was rushing forward, far faster than Kat had ever imagined he could move. The goon let Hale go and raced for his boss, but he was too late. In a flash, Eddie was on the lawyer, and the lawyer was spinning, striking the old man across the head with the metal briefcase. Blood rushed from Eddie's mouth and he stumbled, disoriented, too close to the edge.

"No!" Kat yelled again, but she didn't hear the word. She heard nothing at all. Not the crunch of the rocks. Not the breaking of the barrier as it crumbled at her uncle's back. And Kat didn't hear the screaming that came with the fall—fading with the sound of the water and the cries of the people who stared over the edge.

She didn't hear or feel or say a thing. Her own legs gave way and she was on the ground, damp grass bleeding through her jeans, freezing her, numbing her.

"No," Garrett said. "It's not true. It's a trick. They're con men," he yelled, as if that could explain everything, make it all make perfect sense.

"That man's dead," a bystander said flatly, but Garrett just pushed him aside and stared for himself through one of the cameras trained on the falls below.

"He's . . . He can't be . . ." Garrett stumbled away from the sight, pale as ghost, but Kat kept crawling toward the ledge.

"I'll go get him," she said. "I'll get him and then we can bring him to the hospital. . . ." She stumbled to her feet. "I have to get him."

But she didn't move—couldn't move because Hale's arms were around her so tightly her feet no longer touched the ground.

"Let me go, Hale. I have to go get him and help him up."

"No, Kat. No."

"Let me go!"

"No." Fury faded, and Kat knew Hale wasn't going to let her near the edge.

"I have to get him, Hale."

"No," he said, and held her tighter. "I have you."

"Mr. Garrett," the goon said. "We have to get you out of here."

"He fell," Garrett said.

"Your fingerprints are all over that case, sir, and now that case is lying by his body and covered with his blood. You have to leave. Now."

They didn't seem to care about the crying girl or the crumpled body. They just drove away, wheels spinning, the SUV disappearing into the mist.

CHAPTER 44

There wasn't really a manhunt, not in the traditional sense. No one alerted Interpol. There were no roadblocks or Wanted posters. No one in a position of authority was going to care too much about the death of the king of the thieves.

Sure, the tabloids had all picked up on the news that Reginald Hale had gone over Niagara Falls, and by morning the rumors would be rampant; but for that night, at least, the streets were dark and the stove was cold. Kat couldn't look at it. But she couldn't look away either.

"Kat," Hale told her, "you should get some sleep."

"No." She pushed his hand away.

"Come on. You're going to need your strength tomorrow."

But before Kat could protest, there was a knock on the door.

"That's probably the boys," Hale said, but he was wrong.

Kat knew as much as soon as she heard Natalie's voice say, "Hey, Scoot."

"Go away." He tried to slam the door in her face, but Kat caught the edge, held it there, and glared at the girl on the stoop.

"What do you want?" Kat didn't want to look the girl in the eyes, but she had to.

"I heard about what happened and . . . Are you okay, Kat?" Natalie asked.

"What do you want?" Kat said again.

"I'm so sorry, Kat. And Hale, I never thought my dad would forge a DNR. You've got to believe me."

She reached for Hale's hand, but he pulled it out of her grasp.

"I don't have to do anything," he said, and for a moment, Kat thought he might hit her. "But *you* have to *leave*."

"No, Hale. Listen. I know . . . I know I did a terrible thing, but I never dreamed my father would hurt Hazel."

"Really?" Hale was shouting, and Kat doubted he even knew it. "What did you think he would do?"

"I don't know." Natalie bit her lip. Her voice was barely a whisper. "I just . . . He's not a strong man. He's angry and bitter and . . . You don't know what it's like—being near you. All of you. The Hales. You're larger than life, you know that, right? With your houses and your jets. You have everything."

Hale stood trembling, and Kat thought about the boy in the Superman pajamas. He'd had nothing.

But Natalie talked on. "Then my dad told me about the prototype." She shrugged as if she wasn't sure who or what to believe anymore. "He was so desperate to get out from under your family's shadow, so I said that if he felt the Hales owed him so much, he should do something about it."

"But Hazel fired him," Kat said. She thought about the carbon copy of the letter that she'd found in Hazel's desk.

"Yeah." Natalie nodded. She looked impressed that Kat knew. "He was just going to take the prototype and sell it and . . . no one was supposed to get hurt. No one was ever supposed to die."

"That's the thing about being a criminal," Kat told her. "Nothing ever goes according to plan."

"What do you want, Natalie?" Hale was deflating. It was like the fight was leaving his body, and all that was left was an empty, hollow shell.

"I'm sorry. And I just want to make it right."

"You think you can say you're sorry?" Hale yelled, and Kat knew that it must have felt good. Like crying. He must have wanted to purge all the excess emotion from his body, because he yelled louder. "You think that makes it okay?"

Natalie shook her head. Tears streamed down her face. "No. No. Of course not. I just—"

"What?" Hale yelled. "Tell me why I shouldn't spend the rest of my life trying to destroy you."

"The prototype," Natalie blurted.

"I don't care about the prototype." Hale's voice was flat and cold and even.

"You can still save the company," Natalie said. "You can still do what Hazel would have wanted."

"Don't say her name," Hale snapped. "You don't have the right to say her name."

"I know." Natalie looked at the ground. "But if you want it, then you should know that my dad is meeting with a new

307

buyer. In Switzerland. After . . . what happened . . . he knew he was going to have to disappear, so he decided to sell it. Now. Tomorrow. If you hurry, you can catch him."

"Where is he?" Kat asked.

"Zurich. He's meeting his buyer on the twelve-ten to Geneva. They'll be in the last car on the train."

Hale pushed away from the door and rushed down the hall. Kat couldn't tell if he had calls to make or if he just couldn't stand to be in Natalie's presence one second longer. It didn't matter. For a moment, Kat was alone with the girl from Hale's past, the girl who had been there long before Kat had climbed through his window. Part of her wondered about what might have happened if she had never come and he had never left. Nat might have been perfect for him. For Scooter. But Scooter was gone. And despite everything, Kat felt sorry for Natalie. After all, most girls don't get to choose their families.

"I really am sorry, Kat," Natalie tried one last time, but Kat said nothing. She wasn't in the mood to make peace. "If he ever decides to forgive me . . ."

"He won't," Kat said, and closed the door.

THE DAY AFTER
EDDIE DIED

SOMEWHERE
IN SOUTHERN
SWITZERLAND

CHAPTER 45

When the man in the hat boarded the train, he looked like just another businessman, a banker perhaps. No one would have noticed him at all had it not been for the woman he was meeting. She was the kind of woman people couldn't help but notice.

When she gripped his hand, people glimpsed her perfect nails and long, elegant fingers. When she said, "I'm so happy you called," everyone in the first-class car listened to the light trill of the syllables that drifted up and down, as gentle as the jostling of the train.

"I've reserved a private car," the man said, and led the way; but behind the sliding doors, there was no doubt the mood of the meeting changed.

A big, meaty man followed the pair into the private car

and patted the woman down. She didn't object, however. She raised her hands and waited, perfectly accustomed to such a scene.

And when she was finally free to take a seat, she crossed her long legs. "As I said, I'm so glad you called." The woman smiled. "I'm also glad the terms have changed."

"No, they—"

"Yes," she said flatly, "they have. You wouldn't be here if the price hadn't taken a drop. . . . Fallen off a cliff, so to speak."

The man swallowed hard. "It was an accident."

"I'm sure it was," the woman said. "And I'm equally sure that you can have a very nice life in exile. Now, do you have the device?"

He handed her the case that was on the seat beside him. She removed the prototype and plugged it into her phone, waited for the device to spring to life.

"And the schematics?"

He passed her a jump drive, which she plugged into a laptop. A second later, thousands of intricate formulas and designs flashed across the screen.

"If these are incorrect, my employer will make your retirement most . . . uncomfortable."

Garrett shifted nervously, but said, "They work. I just want them gone. Trust me. I never want to see that prototype again."

"Very well," she said. "You have a deal."

The man reached for his own laptop and logged on to the train's wireless network. Soon the screen bore the logo of one of Switzerland's most elite and secure banks. They each typed in a series of numbers, and a moment later, the woman held out her hand.

"It was nice doing business with you, Mr. Garrett."

The man was sweating and breathing hard.

"Congratulations. You're a very wealthy man," she told him, then placed the jump drive and prototype back into the case, slid her purse onto her shoulder. "Enjoy your retirement."

The train pulled to a stop and the woman stood and sauntered down the aisle, back into the first-class car and out the door. When she crossed the platform, briefcase in hand, the man in the hat was perhaps the only person on the train who wasn't watching. He couldn't keep his gaze off of his computer, clutching the machine with sweaty palms as if his whole life lay inside. And that was perhaps why he was the only person who didn't see the teenage girl and boy who chose that moment to board the train themselves and were soon pushing their way into his private car.

When Garrett saw Hale, a flash of fear crossed his face, but then he actually smiled as he snapped his laptop closed. "You're too late." He gave a low, dry laugh.

Hale was rushing down the aisle as the train began to move, but Kat just stood at the door, wondering what kind of person could watch somebody die and then run for the hills, his only concern how much money he might have for the journey.

"Sorry, Scooter, it's gone." He placed his laptop in his bag and his bag on the seat beside him. "You tried. But it's done."

"You stole it," Hale said.

"I took what I was owed!" the man shouted, and still Kat stood, searching his eyes for any sign of remorse, but all she saw was a cold and empty greed that no amount of money would ever satisfy.

"You think that company is your legacy?" Garrett challenged. "Your birthright? It's a tomb."

"You're not going to get away with this," Kat said, and the man looked at her.

"I'm sorry about your uncle, Miss Bishop. I really am. But let's not forget that I know all about you and your family. If anyone comes asking questions about what happened to Reginald Hale, or your uncle, for that matter, they are going to find a very thick file full of very nasty secrets. Take it from someone who has been cleaning up Hale family messes his whole life: let it go."

"Oh, that's okay." Kat felt the rock and sway of the train, held on to the back of one of the seats to stay upright. "I don't think anyone is going to be too concerned about Reginald, considering he's been dead for fifty years."

"But . . ." The man's eyes went wide and his voice trailed off when the door at the back of the car slid open.

"You mean him?" Kat asked, pointing over her shoulder, and for a moment the attorney was so quiet that Kat had to wonder if Garrett even recognized Uncle Eddie.

Gone were Reginald's clothes and his cane. He'd traded his limp for slightly inferior posture, and there was no way the man walking down the aisle would ever be confused with a member of the Hale family. He looked like a man who missed his stove and his kitchen. But he was also a man who was very much alive.

"You . . ." Garrett muttered. "You're dead. I saw you at the bottom of a cliff."

"Did you?" Eddie asked as, behind him, the door slid open once again and Eddie's twin brother, Charlie, came to stand beside him. "Did you really?"

The man stumbled to his feet. "Get them," he told the guard who sat in the next row. "Stop them."

"See . . ." The goon stood and spoke with a deep Scottish brogue. "I probably shouldn't do that. It would set a terrible example for my boys. Hey"—he looked at Kat—"where are Angus and Hamish?"

"Don't worry, Uncle Roy. They'll meet up with us in a bit. I had a little errand for them." Then Kat seemed to notice the look on Garrett's face. "What?" she asked him. "I thought you knew. . . . I have a *very* large family."

"So?" The man choked out a laugh. "It doesn't change anything. The prototype is gone, and I still know where all the Hale family skeletons are buried. If you try to follow me, your family will regret it."

"No"—Hale stepped closer, leaning over the cowering man—"*you* don't get it." When the train began to slow again, Hale glanced out the window. "This is our stop."

A moment later, several men with badges were walking toward the car. Kat actually waved at the woman leading the group.

"See," she said, "that's *my* friend at Interpol. I told her all about you, and she's here to have a chat."

But Garrett didn't tremble. Instead, he actually huffed. "I'm an attorney, Miss Bishop. I haven't broken any Swiss laws."

Kat smiled. Hale chuckled. The two of them shared an *Oh, isn't he adorable* glance before Hale said, "Then it's a good thing we aren't in Switzerland, isn't it?"

"What . . . what do you mean?"

"There was a problem with the tracks, and we got diverted. We crossed the border into France twenty minutes ago."

Outside, Angus and Hamish waved at their father through the window.

"You know my uncle Roy, but I don't think you've met his sons." Kat pointed at the pair through the glass. "What they do best is blow things up."

"Things like train tracks," Hale said.

"Mr. Garrett?" Amelia Bennett was walking down the aisle toward them. She didn't even glance at Charlie or Eddie. She just gave a little nod to Kat and Hale, and turned her full attention to the man in the hat.

"I have some questions about the death of Hazel Hale, among other things."

That Interpol's senior liaison to the European Union was there that day to handle the matter was something no one really questioned. It was her tip. Her call. And if she chose not to interview the other people on the train, that too was her decision.

So the passengers of the 12:10 to Geneva were free to climb from the car and out onto the platform without a question or a doubt. And no one from Interpol said a word as perhaps the greatest thieves in the world walked out of the station and blew to the far corners of the earth.

CHAPTER 46

Walking toward the private plane with Gabrielle and W. W. Hale the Fifth, Kat should have felt at least a little bit nostalgic. It was a familiar feeling, so she slipped her hand through his arm and tried to enjoy the moment—to tell herself that things were finally back to normal. But then Hale stopped.

"What are you doing?" she asked.

"I'm just trying to enjoy this while it lasts."

"Why?" she said. "Are you planning on an early retirement?"

"No." He shook his head and laughed. "It's just that the jet belongs to Hale Industries, and Hale Industries is over." He sighed. "But on the upside, I guess we're getting ready to find out if you really only love me for my jet."

"I might love you for your jet," Gabrielle said, straight-faced.

He smiled at Kat. "What about you?"

"Yeah," Kat said, nodding. "I guess that *is* the question." She looked up at him, squinting through the bright, clear sun. "So . . . Hale Industries? You really think it's over?"

Hale looked ahead, as if the jet wasn't right in front of them, gleaming like a mirage.

"Without the prototype, yeah. I guess we can sell off all the pieces, but the company won't go on. Funny. I didn't think I'd miss it," he said.

"But . . ."

"I think I might miss the possibility of it."

"I'm your Colgan." Kat didn't know she'd said the words aloud until Hale spun on her, took her small shoulders in his hand.

"What's that supposed to mean?"

"I'm the thing you ran to when you wanted to try another life. I'm your big experiment. But in the end . . . maybe you were always meant to go back home."

"Don't say that. This isn't some experiment I'm doing. I'm not running away."

"Yes, Hale. You are. And that's okay. It is," she said when he gave her a look. "I just need you to know that if you ever want to go back home, you can. I did all this to make sure you always had a home to go back to."

"What are you talking about, Kat?"

"I had to do everything, Hale. I had to *try* everything, so that's why I . . ." Kat trailed off, but she looked at Gabrielle, who whistled.

The door of the jet slid down, but Kat couldn't take her eyes off of Hale. She studied the silent, subtle changes in his expression as the woman from the train walked down the stairs and across the tarmac.

"Hale," Kat said, "I don't think you've ever met Gabrielle's mom. Aunt Irina, this is Hale."

He stared, dumbfounded, at the woman who was opening her arms. Gabrielle ran into them.

"Mama," Gabrielle said, and the pair spoke in rapid French.

Finally, the woman pulled away from Gabrielle and looked Hale up and down, examining him before scolding her daughter. "Oh, Gabrielle, why did you let Kat call dibs on this one?"

"She saw him first," Gabrielle said with a smile.

"You . . ." Hale muttered. "*You* bought the prototype?"

"Well, technically, she conned your prototype. If Garrett hadn't been detained, he would have found that the money that was supposed to be in his account wasn't exactly . . . there," Gabrielle told him. "Funny thing about wireless networks. They can be incredibly insecure."

"Plus, Simon is on our side," Kat said.

"Yes," Irina said. "He is. Now, I believe you've been looking for this." Gabrielle's mom handed Hale a case and slid on her dark glasses. "And now it's yours. If you want it."

"So"—Kat eyed him—"*do* you want it?"

2 WEEKS
LATER

NEW YORK, NEW YORK, USA

CHAPTER 47

The board of directors of Hale Industries usually only met on the first of every month, but that day—like so many days of late—was an exception. The owner was still a minor, and the minor's trustee was sitting in a German prison, awaiting extradition to the United States, so no one was surprised when the board was summoned and the new owner and his family descended on the building that bore their name.

What no one was expecting was the sight of a short teenage girl walking into the room where the Hale family was waiting, as easily as if she owned the place.

"Hello, Kat." Hale's mother smiled coolly. "It's nice of you to come, but I'm afraid Scooter is busy. We're about to go in and see the board—sort out this trustee business. I'm afraid he doesn't have time for *you*."

And there it was, the scowl that Hale's mother had first given at the wake, before her son had the shares and the money and the power. Before Senior and his wife had needed Scooter on their side.

"Oh." Kat's eyes were wide. "So *you're* going to be the new trustees, then?"

"Well, of course we are. We're his parents."

"Actually, Mom . . ." Hale said and pointed to the door, where Marianne stood, a confused look on her face.

"Marianne," Senior said. "I wasn't expecting to see you here."

"Grandma was," Hale said, but his eyes never left the woman's.

"What's that supposed to mean?" Senior asked.

"Well, see," Kat told them, "Hazel always meant to give your son the company. Garrett didn't have to change that."

"Then what did he change?" Hale's mother snapped.

"The trustee," Kat said simply.

Hale walked to his grandmother's best friend and took her hands. "Will you do it?" he asked. "The position comes with a pretty significant annual salary, profit sharing, bonuses, and other perks until I turn twenty-five."

Marianne's eyes were wide. "I . . . I don't understand."

Kat shook her head. "Hazel didn't give you a part of the company, Marianne. She gave you *him*." Kat pointed to the boy beside her. "Or temporary control over his shares, at least."

"No one will blame you if you say no," Hale said, blushing. "I'm not exactly returnable."

"I . . ." Marianne looked dumbfounded. "I can't do this."

"*Hazel* did it," Hale said. "And you were right by her side every step of the way. If anyone can run this place the way she did, it's you." He turned back to the door and said, "And you don't have to do it alone."

He turned the knob to reveal Silas, bow tie and all.

"Sorry I'm late." Silas gave the little laugh that Kat had grown to love so much. "I've been busy in my new lab." He chuckled and held up a small case. "I took the liberty of making a few upgrades to the original Genesis design." He pulled out a new prototype and gave Kat a wink. "I had a most capable assistant."

He handed the device to Hale, then smiled at Marianne, who walked to the leather chair where Hale's grandmother had sat. She ran her hands over the seat back, as if guessing whether or not she might fit.

"You can work as little or as much as you'd like," Hale told her. "But the job is yours. As far as I'm concerned, it was always yours."

"Oh my." Marianne gave Marcus a glance. "Brother?"

"Your mistress has asked something of you, Marianne." He stood up straighter, as if to say it was a matter of pride. "I do not think it is our place to question it."

Marianne nodded slowly.

But Senior was shaking his head. "No. Just no. We've already dealt with one outsider in that position, and look at what that got us. He's my son and he's a minor, and I will be the trustee of my family's company."

"Actually, Mr. Hale," Silas interjected, "a funny thing happened when we were digging around on the servers. We actually found a copy of your mother's will."

"You did?" Senior asked.

Silas reached into his case again and pulled out a document. "Yes, sir. And Marianne was the original trustee. See?"

He pointed to one of the pages. "Those were your mother's wishes."

"No." Senior shook his head. "I don't believe it."

"It's what she wanted." Hale's voice was calm and even. He wasn't trying to con them, Kat could tell. He just wanted to make them understand Hazel—to understand him.

"You're a child," Senior spat.

"I know," Hale said. "But she chose me, Dad. I'm sorry, but it's the truth. She chose me. And she chose Marianne. And you can either support us and help us, or you can leave. It's your call." Hale raised his eyes. "It's always been your call."

Kat wasn't sure what they'd say—what they'd do. She had seen enough people backed into corners to know there was no predicting how they would react. W. W. Hale the Fourth looked at his son like he was little more than a stranger. And Kat felt her heart start to break.

"I don't have to take this." Senior puffed out his chest.

"No, you don't." Hale stepped away. "But if you decide to try, Marianne will know how to find me."

His mother got her purse. His father reached for the door.

"Scooter," he said, by way of good-bye, "have fun with your friends."

But Hale was shaking his head. He put his arm around Kat's shoulders. "She's not my friend, Dad. She's my girlfriend."

Hale's parents must have walked away, but Kat wasn't looking. She was too busy staring up at Hale, trying to see into his eyes and know if he was okay. The sadness that had lingered for weeks was fading, and the boy that held her was the boy she knew. A boy who kissed her lightly.

Silas cleared his throat, and Kat remembered they weren't exactly alone.

"I'm sorry to bother you, Mr. Hale, but there is something we need to discuss before we go in."

"What's that, Silas?"

"Well, the strangest thing happened. You know how Garrett filed the wrong prototype plans with the patent office?"

"Yeah," Hale said, and Kat could tell he didn't understand where Silas was going.

"Well, I called D.C. to see about pulling those plans and starting the patent process all over again, but this is what they sent me back."

The papers he handed to Hale made very little sense to Kat. They were covered with formulas and graphs.

"What am I looking at, Silas?"

"Those are the plans for Genesis." He leveled Hale with a stare. "The *real* plans."

"So . . . Garrett didn't file phony plans after all?" Kat asked, wondering if they'd gone to all that trouble for nothing, but then Silas laughed.

"No, I don't think so. This was with them." He handed a note to Hale.

It seemed there was a problem with the Genesis plans at the patent office. But don't worry. It's been taken care of. After all, there is _always_ a way around.

Welcome to the family.

—BB

"Something wrong, Mr. Hale?" Silas asked.

"No, Silas." Hale slipped the paper into his suit pocket like it was the most precious thing he'd seen since he first stared up at Hazel's fake Monet. "Everything is just right."

There was a knock at the door, and a young assistant popped her head in. "Excuse me, the board is meeting now."

And with that, Silas extended an arm to Marianne, who took it, and together, the two of them walked toward the boardroom, prototype in hand. But Hale didn't follow. For a second he just stood and stared out over his empire. It was like he was lost in a dream when he said, "So, your dad broke into the patent office."

"Yep," Kat told him.

"How many goats am I going to owe him for that?"

"More than you've got, big guy. Way more than you've got."

"Scooter?" The voice stopped him. Marianne was at the door, looking back. "What will you do?" she asked, and Kat thought she sounded . . . like a grandmother.

"Don't worry about me, Marianne." He smiled at Kat, took her hand. "I'll find some way to stay busy."

ACKNOWLEDGMENTS

It would be impossible to write a Heist book without an amazing crew!

First and foremost, thank you to everyone at Disney-Hyperion: Catherine Onder, Stephanie Lurie, the amazing sales, marketing, and school and library teams. And I would be remiss if I didn't offer a special thanks to Lisa Yoskowitz, who suggested the title for this book and gave it such loving guidance in its early days.

Thanks also to Kristin Nelson and everyone at the Nelson Literary Agency, Kassie Evashevski, Whitney Lee, and Jenny Meyer.

As always, I owe a lot to Rose Brock, Jennifer Lynn Barnes, Holly Black, Shellie Rea, and Bob, who were so much help along the way.

And last but certainly not least, I thank my family, especially the Hale Girls, whom I will always love.